THE

PLASTIC

ISLANDS

The Plastic Islands

By

Jerry Cimisi

Novels by Jerry Cimisi

THE NEW MAN, a novel of 9/11
WUHAN DREAMS, The Pandemic Begins

How inappropriate to call this planet Earth when it is clearly Ocean.

—Arthur C. Clarke

All the king's horses and all the king's men will never gather up all the plastic and put the ocean back together again.

—Charles Moore

The sea is the universal sewer.

—Jacques Ives Cousteau

THE

PLASTIC

ISLANDS

1.

We set out for the Great Pacific Garbage Patch in the summer before the pandemic, leaving San Francisco in the bright light of a sun that glinted on the water up to the horizon—the maritime traveler's eternal road. Lost in this shimmering, the coast disappeared before I realized it; I looked back, it was gone. For a moment I thought I saw the pinpoint silhouettes of ascending gulls warped into the vanishing point. It was the first time in my life I had been wholly out of sight of land.

We sought another sort of coast: almost a hologram of an apocalyptic land. One never goes for any length of time even far out in the ocean without seeing garbage; we were headed to a point at which the debris floating on the surface of the Pacific formed surreal, insubstantial, yet persistent islands: The Great Pacific Garbage Patch.

Estimates of its size compared it to various states: overwhelming evidence that the everyday and often essential objects humans had cast off were forming a literal continent.

*   *   *

After some days the castoff artifacts of humankind were noticeably more present than the day before. His leathery face squinting westward, Hurston said, "We're at the edge. But we've got a way to go—days—before the center."

I looked down at a plastic bleach bottle bobbing next to the face of a deteriorating computer monitor (circa 2000 desktop, I guessed), whose intricate interior was partly exposed, water sloshing through its degraded circuitry. The mismatched pair were like some odd, cryptic, fluid sign, sent from the past to this uncertain present.

"Was somebody using the bleach in Taiwan and the computer in Hawaii—or California?" Hurston said rhetorically.

Then almost immediately sighted was a clump of plastic fishing nets, like a dark morass, or the remnants of some ominous creature, if emptied of whatever marine victims they had once ensnared. Discarded nets may be in fact the most prominent detritus of the seas.

Nathaniel Hurston, lean, tanned, hair golden streaked by sun, had been born quite well off, then had made his own small fortune in designing better surfboards and faster sailboats. He had spent his young manhood as a playboy sailor, racing across the Atlantic and Pacific in the sort of competitions that go with that sort of life—and for the sheer adventure. And then he'd had his epiphany, been given a purpose beyond that of taking his pleasure and testing the competition.

One bright calm day he chanced into the Sargasso of the Pacific where we were now headed, the zone into which ocean currents pushed the detritus of the past hundred years into an area that speculation saw as the size of at least Rhode Island, maybe even Texas—or larger, by other accounts—a floating soup of an island of castoff technology. And thus, the playboy of the seas had been shown his destiny.

"It just came to me, like a command," he told me once. Each

age makes the presentation for a calling in the necessary, contemporary way, I suppose.

For all its size, I found it amazing to learn that this plastic island was not thick enough, substantial enough to be seen from space. The Great Pacific Garbage Patch—or Plastic Vortex—had to be discerned from sea level. It became more and more obvious only as one sailed in toward the center, with the debris of humankind bobbing indifferently alongside, stretched beyond and ahead, a vastly increasing school of material corruption.

Hurston had not been the Patch's discoverer by a long shot; as with the ozone layer a generation ago, the Patch—and other areas like it—had been charted for some time. But having come upon this miasma, Hurston, with the fierceness of someone who had comprehended the essence of a horror before most of us, had abruptly resolved to do something about it.

*   *   *

Hurston scanned the sea with binoculars. We were silent. When he put down the binoculars he said, not so much to me as himself, "Can we make a dent in this?"

As a freelancer for a science magazine, the sort that brought quantum theory and ecological questions to a popular audience, I was accompanying Hurston and the small crew of *The Argus* for my own purposes, although they were perhaps not as clearly defined as Hurston's. Let's say it was more for the sake of the color of the story than for Hurston's evangelical conservationism. I was a young woman eager to pursue a direction whose destination I had yet to define.

So, I could be a little critical of those who hewed a clear cut path. When Hurston added, "I'd like to see this gone in a generation," I thought about how the wealthy can afford to leave a telling legacy, while the rest of us....

"Anything's possible," I said, blandly.

He gave that laugh and smile and that weathered happy look that communicated he was going to show you—and anyone else—just what he could and would do. I considered that this made others believe in anything he proposed. I wasn't sure yet how it struck me.

I looked down at our shadows on the deck, as if in considering myself I sought an outer silhouette. I had just straightened my sporadically sported Afro, so my head cast a different shade than it had two months ago.

I said I was young—more truthful to say I'm young*ish*: born in Orwell's year, 1984. My father had been a Black Panther, so the Afro I sometimes wore for years, then straightened, then returned to, then straightened again, was like a periodic homage to a time in which I had never lived but my father's stories made seem historically romantic.

Anyway, so here I was, an African-American scrivener logging the quest conceived by this sun bleached scion of a somewhat privileged class.

Of course, this trip was a baby step—research, sampling, mapping—to figure out just how to accomplish Hurston's legacy. *The Argus*, which looked more like a 19th century ship than one from the 21st, with sails and masts and ropes, elegant in its old beauty, carried the equipment of a technology whose refuse Hurston hoped to eradicate. (And would sometimes give me a sense of historical displacement.)

"Not exactly a posh water view."

Rita Cosgrove, the English oceanographer, joined us on deck. Her outright beauty—great figure and features and thick dark hair—as always made her a presence. Hurston uncharacteristically gave her a frown. It was involuntary. Since the voyage had begun it had been obvious that Hurston regarded Rita (whom he had confided to me as being "sometimes difficult") with a manner of an inner conflict. She was striking and he was attracted to her. She had an innate radar—and subsequent sarcasm—for human foibles. For all his directed energy and drive, Huston was a man who had his insecurities. That was plain. With this Great Pacific Garbage Patch business Hurston was proving himself, proving his worth to himself and to, well, society. But lovely Rita wasn't awed by him. (I, another woman, wasn't either.) Hurston was obviously not comfortable with and not indifferent to Rita; all the more so because he apparently had a fiancé somewhere on shore.

Rita looked at the bottle of bleach and the computer monitor, now receding past us. "Relatively new stuff. Hasn't had time to degrade."

There was that private look in her eyes (when she became all science) as she turned in the direction of our progress. "We'll reach a point, a sort of rim, where it's pretty thick, then the center will have garbage so degraded it'll look clear—like the eye of a hurricane."

She went on to say what she had spoken about before: Rita had a tendency to inform you more than once with her knowledge. The ability to pinpoint the flaws of others doesn't mean you'll be as perceptive about yourself. "It'll be utterly neustonic at the center—"

Neustonic had originally been applied to living things that thrived on or just below the surface of the water—such as flying fish, water striders, the diving bell spider. Now it had become a word also used for plastic on the sea, not just the large pieces we were passing, but the minute particles of plastic that had been broken down by long exposure to the elements, joining in size the world of plankton, and swallowed along with like organisms by various marine life, providing not merely a lack of nourishment but of poison.

A stumbling sound came from the hatch. Media maven Melissa (forgive the alliteration) Connors emerged into the hot light, blandly good looking in typical newswoman style, her bleached blonde hair uncharacteristically tousled. She squinted at us and the debris beyond. Her blue eyes had been altered by contacts into the disturbing inanimate hue of gems. Her phone, dislodged in her clumsy ascent, flew from her and clattered on the deck. Hurston stopped it with his foot.

Melissa cursed as Hurston made as if to kick it back to her. He laughed, stooped and picked it up. "No service," she said, as she grasped it from him.

"I told you—out here—"

"What about that satellite feed?"

"That was just to get you to sign up for the plan," called out another member of our eccentric expedition. Melissa's cameraman—or would it be more correct to say videographer?—Blaise Augustine, was a youngish (yes, it's a useful word) man I saw as climbing with calculation some fantasy ladder of broadcast journalism. Slim, dark haired, not that handsome, with a manner of flippancy and petulance that made you know right away he could not be interested in the sex represented by Rita, myself, and Melissa, he gave his assessment of the newswoman's phone service the obvious meaning of: I could not be taken in like that. –Though ostensibly it was meant to be received as affectionate needling. It was the way in which he often communicated his annoyance with Melissa—an annoyance she usually disregarded as being incapable of unseating her.

In fact, Melissa now pointed past us and shouted to Blaise— commanded him: "Get a shot of that garbage!"

Blaise reacted with resigned alacrity. In another moment he was filming some strips of plastic—as if a plastic lounge chair had been cut up by a giant slicer—that had come to bob alongside us.

I went down below with Hurston, leaving Rita, the insistent newswoman and calculating cameraman to take in the periphery of the Patch.

No, *The Argus* was not glutted with females. There was Rory Chapman, a researcher for a major plastics company in the southwest, a firm allegedly in the forefront of creating biodegradable plastic. A tall, laconic type, he looked more like the old stereotype of a cowboy than a scientist.

Then there were the two Central Americans (Mesoamericans I liked to say), Emile and Jorges, who fulfilled the more sailorly and menial tasks of the ship. They might have been the stereotypes here: Hispanics toiling for the descendants of the culture that had once invaded their New World. Both short and squat, they had those common Mesoamerican bodies and faces, reminding me of Mayan glyphs. Their dark lively eyes occasionally rested contemplatively on Rita, then on Melissa, and perhaps me, too—out of consistency and politeness.

I had watched them watch Hurston discoursing on his vision of redemption from plastic, bearing the expression I'd often seen on Hispanics serving the public at minimum wage jobs. Though I'm sure Hurston paid Emile and Jorges well. He could not let himself seem the type to exploit a worker. Readers of the politically correct persuasion will see ethnic bias here: I believe I'm just reporting. Two nights ago I had turned from a beautiful sunset to see Emile toss a plastic water bottle over the side, not even taking in the aesthetic look of its bob on the sunset-colored sea as he left to go down below. It was no reach to conclude that the planet Earth had billions of Emiles (of various ethnicities), not so much bereft of the ecological Word, but indifferent to its exhortation that one bit of plastic so idly tossed could actually destroy the immemorial links of biosystems.

I watched the conclusion of the sunset and some of its star-lit aftermath (out at sea, the stars were glorious) with more sadness now than appreciation. How far could we inch our detritus into the universe? Well, we were limited by the confines of the planet, but who knew what the future would enable us to inflict? With some increasingly absurd battle between the Hurstons and the Emiles? With the Hurstons needing to employ the Emiles? With observers like me using the excuse of reporting to condemn, but not make it aright?

2.

We sailed on, the heat and light continuing, the plastic floating debris increasing—from shards of unrecognizable objects to plastic outdoor tables and spoons. The silent presence of these castoff artifacts floating in the midst of nowhere was like a banal visual epitaph to a civilization that Rory, the more reserved and solitary of us, randomly fished out of the water, while Rita periodically inserted a long slim rod into the ocean to ascertain the character of the currents. Rita once said to me, "The sea is like the body of Earth, the currents its temperature—well, energy."

I noted Hurston watching Rita repeatedly bend over the railing of the ship, the necessary posture of her inquiry a perhaps not unconscious sexual taunt. Our captain did penance by listening to Rita explain the complex factors that influence currents. When I remarked, "That's a lot to take in," Hurston, either ignoring or innocent of my double *entendre*, said, with apparent sincerity, "If I expect to change this, I've got to know."

If I responded to the male's expected attraction to the uber-female with both resignation and amusement, Melissa was so often demandingly in Hurston's face, determined to cast him as the rich man, the rugged rich man, out there doing good; and in this blatant translation of Hurston from playboy to environmental warrior, the newswoman expected—I knew this in my gut—Hurston's appreciation. Oh, I won't say *she* was attracted to our captain; she merely wanted to be the one—whether male or female—that was most at the center of attention.

Her persona and profession were on the surface a paradox; she was supposed to be giving center stage to others, the newsmaker or makers of the day, but what her psyche really aspired to was to be the name more important than the news. Then I had to ask myself: Did I desire fame? I saw myself as toiling in more thoughtful realms: readable, but not sensational science: knowledge and, consequently, truth. Well, at least knowledge. Perhaps, I considered one afternoon, while watching a jumbled vista of plastic debris spread across the ocean, I could achieve some wider success, by being, yes, pure and wholly honest in my communicating—without the broadcast gimmicks of Melissa. But was I ready to accept the vanity of this purity?

Purity—impurity. That last word hung in my psyche, like the insistent sun. What was this life but one creeping impurity, like the silent debris that bobbed alongside *The Argus*, far outward, toward the horizon?

*   *   *

There was a brief stretch of bad weather, a few hours' worth, but the thickness and fury of the storm, the wild agitation of the sea, the pelting rain, the thunder and lightning—made these hours seem long. I had brief flashes of worry: could *The Argus* be heaved over by the wild waters? Hurston caught my look, read my concern, and told me he'd been through much rougher seas. He didn't have to assuage Rita, who seemed to actually enjoy the rough weather, standing on deck for a good while as the ship tilted, the rain and thunder raged and lightning crackled. Had my assessment been unkind I would have said she enjoyed displaying how her T-shirt was plastered to her torso, but I had the sense that something in her psyche intimately connected with the wild ocean world.

Melissa pushed Blaise out into the deluge to get all the footage he dared—while she, the staunch newswoman, spoke before Blaise's technological eye: "In the midst of this philanthropic research expedition we are reminded of the fury of Nature!" I'll admit her energy sounded sincere. And at the very word "Nature!" the sky thundered and Melissa turned her hooded, drenched head, and the camera turned that way too, to the lightning that smoked viciously across the sky, perfectly on cue.

Not caught on camera was the occasional shard of some plastic object, or an entire object being thrown onto the ship by the storm—or, as happened twice, flung in the air across the deck and never landing on the ship at all. One of the objects that did land was—as if some spirit were mocking the efforts of Hurston's expedition—a toilet seat, stained green by the sea and distressed with cracks by the sun. It duly landed not far from Hurston and he picked it up, laughed a laugh that was lost in the sounds of the storm, and held the oval up in the rain soaked air, like trophy. He was about to toss it back to the raging ocean, but out of nowhere Rory grabbed Hurston's wrist, who looked at the scientist with a start.

"I'd like to examine that," he said to Hurston, who gave another storm-drowned laugh. Of course: the researcher needed his toilet seat.

Rory smiled too, received the seat, and went down below. I followed. Emile and Jorges were there, dry and calmly drinking coffee. I accepted a cup. "You like the rain?" Emile said to me, half laughing at my soaked appearance.

"It's not just rain, but a storm," I said with logical inanity. "But I like to see...." My words drifted off. I could never explain to anyone the satisfactions of my curiosity, of my observations.

For the first time I got in conversation with Emile and Jorges. I had had the feeling from the beginning they regarded me as apart from the crew, for the dual reason that I was a reporter and because of my race. Both men had been itinerant landscapers in the Hamptons, had taken extra work in cleaning someone's yacht docked in Sag Harbor (the town whose 19th century morals had made Melville's cannibal Queequeg uneasy), and had gradually drifted into the sailing life. Emile told me he'd been in America since a teenager. Jorges had come north a bit more recently. "Not an easy journey," he'd told me blandly.

I said to Emile—trying to make it offhand, almost joking, "I saw you throw a plastic bottle in the water the other night. Don't you know that's what this whole thing is about?"

Emile gave one of those polite smiles that say the bearer is forced to do so. "One bottle from me— If they put water in plastic bottles what are people supposed to do?"

I pointed out there was a recycling bin on board. Jorges laughed. I didn't like the laugh. There was a cruelty to it, and it felt directed at me. Emile just mumbled, "I remember—next time." But perhaps his expression said something else.

So ended that conversation.

I heard Blaise clambering down from the deck, cursing, strands of his hair clinging to his forehead. He was soaked. "Her highness releases me—when it's almost over." He went to have a beer.

I went back on deck. The rain wasn't heavy now, just a fine insistent spray. I did not see "her highness," but I did see Rory looking at the sea and sky with a transport I felt immediately, too. To the east the sky was still dark and interlaced with lightning, but westward it was clearing. The sun, emerging from the progress of the storm, threw its light over the retreating dark grey masses of the clouds in beautiful shafts. And there, of course, was a rainbow.

Rory, with whom I probably hadn't exchanged 50 words since we'd set out, smiled at me and gestured to the sky. "Beauty at the end of the storm."

Prettier than a toilet," I said.

He laughed. "It is." I had thought Rory the dry researcher who would not have ever noted any beauty outside of his polymers.

"Unfortunately there remains—" He gestured to the surface of the ocean now, where the scattered garbage of the Patch's periphery floated.

I gave an expression of agreement and said nothing. We stood there for a few minutes, quiet, looking at both the heavens and the bobbing garbage. Rory broke this reverie by scooping up some plastic debris right alongside the ship. In the net at the end of a long shaft—like a very long butterfly net—was the torso and one arm and smashed-in head of a doll, one eye concave and distended. This damaged human simulacrum disturbed me; and it bothered me how Rory drew it from the net as if this bit of garbage had not been a child's toy and had, at some time, been attached to innocent emotions.

3.

Not much later that afternoon, when the storm clouds had receded past the eastern horizon, we had the shock of seeing a small boat come into view in the west. It was the sort of boat you'd see near shore, not in the middle of the ocean. A man was in it: fiftyish, with disarrayed clothes, unruly grey-brown hair and a wild expression. He waved at us frantically.

We came alongside him and Hurston began to help him onto the deck; he needed an assist from Rory. The surprising voyager was a little heavy. His white bulky shorts showed thick sunburned legs. He was a bit out of breath, his eyes red from the sun and some interior effort—or fear, I thought.

Hurston said, "Where the hell did you come from?"

The man's quickly blurted reply seemed to overlap the question. "We caught your radio. From the islands—"

Before Hurston could say it, Rita did: "What islands? There's nothing—"

He took a deep gulp of breath and waved behind him. "The plastic islands. Smith's. The storm—"

Hurston: "*What* islands?"

The man sighed, as if drawing himself in. He had a chubby face, as if it had soaked up too much water. Then he laughed and coughed. "Smith's plastic islands." He quickly added. "This must sound crazy to you. I'm Charles Langhorn." He stuck his hand out tentatively to Hurston, who shook it cautiously. At this point I think the beset voyager seemed to all of us more apparition than real

Though the name sounded familiar to me, but I couldn't say why. And Melissa abruptly pinpointed him in her social catalogue: "I knew I knew you! I interviewed you last year!"

Langhorn squinted at her with an odd relief. "My God, you did. Six degrees of separation."

Melissa, displaying her knowledge of matters beyond all of us, announced: "Charles Langhorn. The famous art critic." She had to use the word "famous"; after all, *she* had interviewed him. But then she demanded: "What's the plastic islands? Who's Smith?"

Langhorn said, very evenly, as if Melissa, for all her proud knowledge, might not grasp the name: "Arturo Smith. The artist."

Again Melissa responded with recognition; I don't think it was feigned. "Arturo Smith? Where? Here?"

Now I placed Langhorn: the critic of the day who told the public what was good in the matter of art, and why. Perennial guest on National Public Radio, PBS stations, etc. I was hardly an aficionado of the arts, and I was not inclined to offer obeisance to so-called experts in any field. But, if I was hardly up on the latest in the art world, I did know about Arturo Smith.

"The conceptual artist," I said to Melissa.

"I know, I know." She assured me. To Langhorn she again demanded. "Smith's here?"

The critic gestured to the west. "His new project: the plastic islands."

I don't know if the others imagined as correctly as I did just then. The immediate future would verify my hunch.

*   *   *

Arturo Smith had been born with the much more common name of Arthur Smith. He accurately realized that he might make more of a splash in the art world if one of his names sounded more uncommon. The simple displacement of one letter from his first name and one letter added it made Arthur into Arturo—and had made this name recognized in that borderland of art and showmanship, creating (with a good many helpers), very large art: Egyptian-type designs across a mile of the Egyptian desert (designs which he allowed the sands to eventually erode), outlining the entire coast of a small island with flags, hanging a mesh of lights from the Golden Gate Bridge (I had seen a postcard of this "installation" before we'd left Frisco), and other efforts in this vein. His art was one of scale; though he was hardly creating monuments. As I said, the pharaonic designs were effaced by the shifting sands, the shoreline of flags in place for two weeks, and the abstract web work of lighting on the bridge in place for ten days. The permanence of his art was in the films and photographs of the work, enough of a record to ensure retrospectives (as if exhibitions once removed) at various prestigious museums. Some had accused Smith of pursuing novelty more than art, and one critic had said, "He is the epitome of our time's addiction to quantity—hence size—over quality." At any rate, when Langhorn spoke about "plastic islands," I instantly got the picture of what was going on. I don't know if Melissa did, or even her ladder-climbing assistant, who exclaimed, "I did my thesis on his work!" And while Rita seemed on the verge of her perpetual sardonicism, the expression on Hurston's face was confused—and apprehensive: as if he had abruptly ascertained a new sort of pollution upon his ocean. The ocean he needed to purify.

*   *   *

About an hour and a half before dark we reached the first of the plastic islands.

It seemed the debris of the sea we had sailed upon had risen from being cast off random objects to creations intelligently formed—masses from the size of a boat to a football field: floating, fused masses of plastic construction Arturo Smith had designed and supervised. Some were fairly level, at most a vague bump of topography, others had been formed with irregular vertical heights, like some post-apocalyptic frieze caught in the moment of melting.

This might have seemed too surreal to be reality—but I saw the shadows on the water that some of their plastic heights cast; if a thing casts a shadow it is real.

I think we were all struck by this spectacle—and creation. Hurston, in fact, was struck into silence. He squinted; his face looked almost pained. Melissa, as always, intended to make the most of this surreal vision; she charged Blaise with "Get this! Get everything!" While the cameraman, it seemed, if accepting orders, was struck with a sort of apprehension. He had been prepared for the boredom of the pollution of plastic debris. But now the genius of Blaise's college thesis had abruptly placed enigmas before him amidst the most nether realms of the ocean. I thought that unconsciously he was realizing there was something he had missed back in college in regard to Smith's psyche. Rita, lovely Rita (yes, you had to think too often of that Beatles' song) was smiling; perhaps she was pleased at this bizarre novelty so unexpectedly placed upon the matrix of her currents. Rory stared from the islands to Langhorn, trying to make some human connection—or any connection really— between these masses of polymers and their creator; though of course he was looking to the wrong man. (Perhaps he suddenly sought a critic's explanation.) The actual creator, it turned out, was at the edge of the large, flat-bumpy island, football field-size, a tall, thin, white-haired man who waved at us; we might have been some casual and wholly anticipated company at some resort isle. Emile and Jorges looked inscrutably upon Smith's world. Their Mayan faces had seen nothing like this in the Hamptons. They were unsure of how such strangeness would affect the accepted toil of their lives.

Well, one never knows how one is to be marked by the twists and turns of existence.

Hurston snapped out of uneasy reverie and commanded Emile and Jorges to help in guiding the 19th century-looking *Argus* to an apparent dock on the plastic island. As we had neared, Smith had pointed out its location and walked towards it. There was a lightness, a spring in his step that was the manner of a happy madness, a gadfly.

Melissa, not wanting to be on the periphery of anything, was posed on the railing of the ship as the island drew up (and the waving, calling, figure of Smith, like something in a cartoon, grew more defined), the newswoman earnestly spouting to her public as Blaise filmed—"In the midst of a sea of plastic, of generations of human garbage, suddenly our perspective of such debris is transformed by the work of the controversial artist Arturo Smith—"

She wasn't wrong about a jolt to one's perspective. Docked at the island, the few seconds of greeting, at Smith being both happy and amused (and some other reaction that escaped me) at seeing Langhorn with us—these few seconds were felt by me as an elongated stretch in which I slipped from the rhythms of *The Argus* to some other world whose intrinsic nature had a lot more to it than the half abstract, half concrete constructions of an artist who wanted his work seen large on Earth.

In fact, I felt myself in a place literally like no other place on the planet.

It was a transition further deepened by the appearance of others, Smith's crew of workers. It was obvious they were from at least a half dozen countries. From dark, dark black bodies to very fair skinned (say a half dozen continents, not countries), both men and women, from youths who were probably no more than twenty to those who seemed as old as the artist himself. I guessed Smith around seventy. This disparate army emerged from every cranny and plain of the islands, the island Smith was on, as well as the others nearby, each man and woman as strangely silent and controlled as Smith was loquacious; he was introducing himself as one knowing he needed no introduction, and who happily took in our names, as if he were affixing the presence of invited guests. At any rate, his animation, contrasting with the cautious greeting of *The Argus'* crew (well, Melissa had her own sort of animation), and the quiet emergence of Smith's workers made me think the whole scene the maddest drama abruptly played upon one of Dali's melted landscapes.

The landscape upon the seascape: melted, hardened plastic of all textures, colors, roughness, smoothness—even, yes, scent, The smell of old plastic, new plastic. I could believe— and so quickly—that it was as natural to walk on plastic as on the earth. This was indeed another world brought down upon this one.

Hurston was saying to Smith, "Your friend here, Mr. Langhorn—"

Smith burst in: "Charley was just too *upset* with the storm!" He slapped Langhorn on the shoulder. The heavyset critic winced. "Just because *his* little island toppled over he thought it was all—gone!" Langhorn frowned, looking scolded. –And that seemed the disguise of an expression that communicated something else.

*   *   *

In that last hour of light Arturo Smith walked us about this largest of the plastic islands, plainly pleased at our presence. He had a delicate face with thin, almost unwrinkled skin; you could see tiny veins just below the surface. He made me think of some 19th century New England preacher gone pleasantly mad with his devotions. "It was such an obvious *find* for the art I most liked to do: all this garbage on the water. I don't remember exactly how it hit me: I could condense it into islands of sculpture. I've always looked at sculpture as something larger than the definition we all accept without thinking about it: something—even if it's bigger than life size—contained in a narrow field of vision. Well, we accept architecture as art—though it also must be functional; we have to use buildings. I wanted to make something large that…didn't have to be functional. Though then again, this island here," he gestured with palms outward, "serves as base, shelter— Apart from art." He nodded to Hurston. "Raise awareness, as you are doing."

Hurston had briefly told Smith the purpose behind *The Argus*. Now our captain's response was: "Awareness, yes, but to do something ourselves, too. To get things done, you don't need an army."

Smith laughed. "You're saying I have one."

Hurston was placating. "Well…a big staff."

"What I mean to say is if more and more people are sympathetic to what you're doing, you'll have less obstacles in your way."

Hurston had to ponder his response to that. He seemed to be treading on this plastic world with the utmost caution. I got the feeling Hurston felt Smith was usurping his territory. He simply replied, "That helps, yes."

As I've said, this largest of the plastic islands was mostly level, with the sort of bumpiness that made me think of the result from leaving plastic inside an oven. And, of course, that was how the islands had been created: with heat. At a question from Rita, Smith began to describe the process: "I came out here with one small boat and a welding torch…." And what he had fused together grew larger, along with the small army (that word again) of workers with torches gathering the debris of technology into the first island, then using it as a "base for the work that would not just be here," proclaimed Smith, "in the middle of the Pacific, but which collectors—let's say benefactors" (he laughed, as if making fun of his own commercial needs) "—would place along the coasts of continents, rivers, harbors—"

As if he had had it all timed and staged, we stopped, on the other side of the island now, before two half completed "sculpture" islands that were shaped like chess pieces: a rook and a knight. They were each a mixture of colors; each had a base as wide as they had been worked high. Beyond them the sun was setting. I had the ominous feeling—no, not quite the right word; a feeling of displacement, in which, alongside an appreciation for what Smith had done (even if I hesitated to call it "art") was the certainty that this was a sort of madness— if a madness not to be disdained. If you piece together some bits of garbage it can be called "tramp art." If you do it on the scale of Smith it demands, well, a larger attention. The author of *Moby Dick* had said there was a purpose to writing about large things.

To steady myself I look again to shadows: the shadows of the giant rook and knight cast upon the water…shapes that had some "intent" beyond the game pieces they replicated.

4.

There were living quarters on the plastic islands—of plastic, of course—and Smith invited us to bunk there; but it was not merely Hurston's desire that we sleep on the now familiar *Argus*, but the way the rest of us felt, too. Certainly I would have felt odd—I won't say uneasy—sleeping in plastic land. Though Melissa lingered (and that meant Blaise had to also), as she wanted to interview Smith right away. Blaise had kept his camera going throughout our tour of the island, and Melissa had interposed her questions, though she seemed more reserved and even thoughtful then I'd ever seen her. I realized she had become a caricature in my mind—and she could be indeed that. But she did have an intelligence. It was just that her psyche had bent that intelligence a certain way.

"Well," said Rita to Hurston when we were all back on board, "strange things upon the sea."

Guardedly, Hurston said, "It's good, though—what he's doing."

Rory said, "So you think a great plastic chess piece will be floating next to the Statue of Liberty?"

"Some other part of New York Harbor, I could see," was my offering. I gave a facial shrug as Hurston turned on me, wanting to know if I were serious.

Rita said, "There was something off the island, under construction—like steps of a pyramid—a ziggurat."

I had noticed it, pyramid or ziggurat, just before sundown and hadn't really thought it was supposed to be a definite shape.

Rita went on: "A ziggurat. He's going to sacrifice his workers when he's done."

As if discounting this only on practical grounds, Hurston

said, "I don't think he's going to be done soon. He's got an ocean of plastic."

*   *   *

Sleeping on *The Argus* that night was different from other nights. I realized it was more than knowing we were docked alongside a plastic island. Throughout the voyage there had been a certain tangible sound of the ocean, the vast ocean utterly surrounding the ship in every direction; now the mass of the plastic island altered that "surround-sound," blocking a portion of the waters. (I no longer missed land.) I can't say it kept me up, but there was, for me, a somewhat uneasy drift into sleep.

As softly persistent as the altered sea was the murmur of conversation between Hurston and Rita. I don't know how long they talked into the night; nor did I know how long Melissa had kept Smith (and hence Blaise) into the depths of an interview. Though I was sure Smith, a man of large, obtrusive works, was glad of all this attention. Yes, that was how he struck me: more showman than artist. Perhaps there is some level of artistry in crafting an artistic public face in one's time. Warhol was the master at this. An old friend of mine, I should say a friend who is elderly, also a journalist, had both interviewed Warhol and observed him, with friends, and with the public, and had concluded that the white-wigged droll icon of a certain peculiar time had been so successful because he *did not* delude himself with pretensions. He did not try to be the 20th century Michelangelo or Van Gogh, but had simply wanted to produce art that was very, very commercial. (Once when asked, "What is art?" Warhol had replied: "A boy's name.") Others who had proceeded or followed in his vein and who had seen themselves as creative geniuses had failed because they had believed their own lies—let's say their own

PR. "To manipulate others requires a certain honesty with oneself," my friend had said. He'd been one of those East Coast liberal newsmen, almost a stereotype, whose peers had been Woodward and Bernstein, and who had passed from the mortal veil midway through the war in Iraq, a sort of irregular mentor for a young lady who had been drawn to his avuncular crustiness and well of experience, and whose lessons were usually not deluded by his own persuasions.

Strange, or not so strange, how falling asleep by Smith's plastic island brought me thoughts of Andy Warhol, a deceased friend who had been an early signpost, and even the useless war in Iraq. The whole world, whether inner or outer, is never far from us....

*   *   *

I awoke in the dimness of the cabin and went slowly up to the deck, wincing in the bright light. It was hardly late, but the summer sun was high and sharp and hot. I did not see any of the others on deck, but I did see, here and there, figures on both the large plastic island and its lesser, irregular renditions. And I saw—and couldn't understand why I hadn't seen this yesterday—that stretching in a curve that went into the sea-bright distance on both sides of this main island, were many, many plastic islands: a veritable archipelago of plastic islands. They seemed both surreal and natural on this great ocean. Of course, they could not have been created overnight. I thought my powers of observation had been deplorably lacking late yesterday; I had only noted a few islands other than the big one. Perhaps there had been a sea haze.... Or perhaps the surprise of Smith's world, of its novelty had made me incapable in the last hours of yesterday to take this all in. I shook my head, as if to clear my eyes and senses, my thoughts, too, and looked out again on the archipelago...then turned to see Rory coming toward me.

With a glance to the archipelago, he said, "I guess it's the sort of art you can't keep in a museum."

That morning I wasn't replying to statements about art. "So—does it give you another perception about plastic?"

He smiled as his gaze swept along the islands. "No. I think about plastic—I study plastic—at its most intrinsic levels. Whether it's a plastic spoon or a plastic island.... I'm interested in the aggregate effect of all this plastic, of course, but—"

He was relieved of further explanation by the appearance of Melissa who joined us: sleepy-eyed, holding a cup of coffee before her chin, as if she wanted its hot steam to complement this hot air and light—or as if it were a heat she could control. She wore a thin white robe, carelessly (or artfully?) opened to show a good deal of cleavage. Her hair, untidy from bed, actually looked attractive, less artificial; and she had a softer, and less aggressive look in her eyes. If she appeared on her news programs like this, her dominating alacrity might seem sensual.

"Long night?" said Rory.

"Yes. We talked a while…" She didn't look at us, but out on the plastic archipelago and the vast ocean and sipped her coffee. She actually seemed reflective, not needing an audience. God, that was exactly it: reflective. I felt mildly astonished.

I said, "So what do you think about all this? Fantastic? Or ridiculous?"

And she smiled and looked at me in a genuine way. "Both, probably." Another sip, and another gaze about—as if expecting to catch something she might miss otherwise. "Today he's going to show me around a little more. Any of us, he said, if we're interested."

Again, I was surprised, at her offer to the rest of us to come in on this, even if it was Smith who had extended the invitation. The fact that she wasn't keeping the invitation all for herself more than intimated other aspects of Melissa I had not divined.

Rory also seemed to be studying Melissa with surprise and new interest. Though perhaps it was more because she was suddenly projecting an easy attractiveness that might draw most men. Or was it, I suddenly thought, just another of her "on the air" personae? But, as I said, she seemed genuine that morning, with her robe and coffee and gemstone eyes that grew less sleepy, taking in the panorama one ageing artist had created in the midst of debris and primeval ocean.

*   *   *

So, by midmorning, all of us, including the plainly dubious Emile and Jorges, were on tour with Smith, leaving the main island—which Rita had dubbed "Gilligan's Island"—to the small islands, that surreal archipelago. I saw it all more clearly, closely, more minutely.

As for Rita's sardonic appellation: "I used to watch reruns of this when I was a kid. It seemed even more exotic and ridiculous on the BBC. Ginger goes on a three hour tour and she has all those gowns."

I had watched reruns of this cult, campy classic, too. The marooned crew of *The Minnow* (as mismatched as our crew) always receiving other cast off visitors who somehow got off that uncharted island, while the Skipper, Gilligan, et al. never could. Those visitors included what would now be considered offensive stereotypes of natives from nearby islands who spoke in nonsensical gibberish and were conveniently superstitious. My father would remark, "They have to use the savages to make the white people both threatened and smart. I shouldn't let you watch this nonsense." But his conclusion was the show was too stupid to take seriously.

*   *   *

When I saw a huge, plastic propeller rendered so that its blades were like the slim leaves of palm trees, I thought, that's it: there were no trees here, not even plastic pots with vegetation. Not that there weren't some signs of vegetable life. Here and there—giving evidence that earth, not just water, is ubiquitous—even here in the midst of the ocean there were small patches of dirt, gathered in crannies on the plastic islands, dirt borne by air or the clothes of the workers, and in this dirt had settled seeds, borne as indifferently and randomly as the dirt, and without care, had sprouted. It was like when you see thin plants growing out from the cracks of concrete in a city. But these were stray, neglected visitors among the plastic flora.

There were so many impressions.... Some of the islands of the archipelago were connected by stout ropes, as if ships strung together, some with a network of ropes, making a veritable bridge of ropes, giving us passage from one island to the other; some we had to visit by use of a small boat (which Smith jokingly referred to as *The Titanic*).

One of the most striking of the islands was one almost wholly of computer parts. It was at some distance from Gilligan's Island, so I could excuse myself for not noticing it before, as striking as it was—and its aspect did not come into full view until we were much closer to it.

*   *   *

As if the computer monitor bobbing alongside *The Argus* a few days before had been a sign, a herald, the isle was a pile of parts of the computer world we'd entered in the last century: it looked like some mad, deranged head, with computer screens for eyes, multifaceted eyes, like an insect's, seeing—or reflecting—a chaos of perspectives. It didn't appear a whole, complete face, atop a base of plastic, but like a face half risen out of the sea—either a face emerging from a plastic morass, some alien intelligence coalescing into features, or like a face losing itself, melting down, no longer in control of its own borders. It suggested both a "spiritual" ascent and descent. I understood when Smith said he called it "Janus."

But I think it made all of us uneasy to look at. Like the apparent ziggurat, there was (never mind its technological components) a primal visceralness to it that was far apart from our own; and more than the suggestion of, well, an intelligence, alien and separate.

It was on this island or isle on which the face/head took up most of the space that Rory Chapman remarked to Smith, "I've noticed…that a lot of the plastic you use—like these monitors, too—don't seem much affected by water at all. As if they hadn't been floating around long—or not at all."

It seemed as if Smith did not want to respond. There was a look in his eyes, the nonchalance of a reply that might have said, "You really think so?"—but it was a thin manner laid before a wariness. What he actually did say, vaguely, was, "It depends."

Melissa, who of course with the aid of Blaise was filming this all for posterity, abruptly said, "Arturo was going to tell us something about that later, I think." As she smiled at "Arturo" (Melissa would want to stress that familiarity) I thought she had gleaned the night before some information from Smith that was pertinent to his whole project and of which we did not know.

Rory said, "Well, I'll be interested in hearing about it."

Smith gave no expression.

Rita said, "I'd be interested in hearing about your ziggurat." She gestured to the other end of the archipelago, where the half completed structure floated.

Smith brightened. "Oh, one of my South American workers gave me the idea—a student of pre-Columbian history. I've put him in charge of it. You'll meet him. Alfredo."

On this tour, more extensive than the day before, some of Smith's workers paid absolutely no attention to us (though it seemed an indifference that indicated it was deliberate; they were in fact noticing and decided not to appear they did), and others looked at us with silent scrutiny. A few were very friendly and smiled; others gave us a wary greeting. Perhaps they knew they were involved in something strange, and did not want the judgement of outsiders. And if it was a greeting in English, it was apparent English was not the native language of any of them. Smith, honored—and funded by—the American art world, was doing his Next Big Thing with the labor of the non-American world. Yes, most of the world isn't American, but you know what I mean. I had the thought—I was doing a lot of interior musing since encountering the plastic islands—that here, in the midst of this Sargasso of refuse, was a sort of post-colonial endeavor, some remnant of the heirs of the European (and for its first two centuries the U.S. was almost wholly that) still requiring the labor of "others" to bring forth an ideal. I wouldn't say that was *exactly* what Smith was doing, and he didn't seem like an intentional "exploiter" (his exploitation was in making his own trend in the art world), but I was certain there was an echo here of something unpleasant, if receding in time (but still not all that distant). An unconscious echo, probably. I reflected that perhaps this Alfredo's inspiration—suggestion?—about the ziggurat had been at least an unconscious rebellion against

Smith's "echo": pre-Columbian, pre-European, when the first natives of the Americas slaved to raise their own venal heights.

5.

Returning to Gilligan's Island, I saw Langhorn in the distance, at the "shoreline," looking toward one section of the archipelago—though his posture suggested a man looking beyond what he was seeing. He had not accompanied us on the tour; of course, he'd seen it all before. But it suddenly struck me then that the chubby critic had been very much in the background since we'd returned him to Smith's plastic islands. We have the ability if we want to replay especially the recent past with a different focus. And focusing on what had been Langhorn's manner, it seemed to me he had not been happy. Not happy for some reason with what Smith was doing? Had the storm been an excuse to escape? That wasn't logical, I knew—setting out in a small boat in the middle of the Pacific, and being hardly a sailor.

I joined him at the plastic shoreline. It was a shoreline artfully constructed. There wasn't an abrupt end like a raft, but gradually tapered into the water. Langhorn barely gave me a glance; I don't think he was pleased at my company. I opened with, "Well, this is definitely strange art."

His look might have told me I was being ridiculous. But I sensed that was a guise for conflicts within himself. I added, "So what do you think of it? His magnum opus?"

The critic sighed. He gave me a weak smile. "It's unusual, of course. In fact, it's an achievement—you have to say. Vast…." The word trailed off, as if he wanted to modify that with something else, but was too cautious, too unsure. His eyes blinked in the light. That was what was coming across from him: uncertainty. It was apparent size could not excuse everything. I considered that critics never seem unsure, ambivalent. At least in public. They would never make the normal comment, "I'm not sure if I like it…" –which is a way of expressing the fact that some things both draw and repel. Anyway, Langhorn did continue after a pause, saying, "I've seen so much…art" (as if he were not sure all that seeing had indeed been directed at "art"); "sometimes it becomes—crazy." He smiled with eyes willfully widened against the hot sun as we stood on that artificial shore, as if to show he mocked his own statement, or appeared to.

"Crazy?" I wanted to fix him on that word.

"I mean—" He sighed again, and looked outward again to the waters of the Pacific Garbage Patch and Smith's archipelago. "So much, so many efforts—to express…?" He left the question like something hot and torpid in the breeze of the sea, like the grasp of an instinct he would let dangle without really confronting it.

"Don't tell me you're reaching the state of wisdom where you're questioning the nature of art?" I made this light; I would allow him to mirror that levity or make it more grave.

"I don't know if what I'm thinking is important itself."

"Everything we think is important—at least to ourselves." But did I really believe that?

He said, "I came here when there were only a few of the islands. I'd been in Vietnam, Ho Chi Minh City—"

"The old Saigon."

"Yes. Reviewing an exhibition of artists who were part Asian, part American, or European—"

"East meets West."

"Yes. There was—the cliché—the expected 'post-colonial' art. Some good work." (Interesting how I had just been thinking on matters neo-colonial.) "And some bad work that could only be 'accepted' because it was supposed to be making political statements." And then abruptly he said, "There's something political about this—" He made a gesture to the archipelago. "But I can't explain it to myself."

"That he's using refuse for art?"

"No, not the method, not the means...."

"So the medium isn't the message?"

He laughed. "I'd forgotten that old—truth. I was a child when that was still going around. You *weren't* around—"

"No."

"It's amazing when you think of it—so many things happen before one was born."

I laughed. "You expect to be around for the Big Bang?" He chuckled too, at this absurdist tack, at his comment and mine. I said, "So about this—something nags at you."

He frowned. He was undecided to go further. "I'm not the purist, but—Smith's project: this *art*.... It's supposed to be recycled garbage from the ocean. At least half of it—the plastic—" (he gave a sweeping wave) "he buys."

"Buys?"

There's a big industry—especially in Asia—selling plastic debris. Especially computers. That island—that head—that head of computers: three quarters—maybe more—of that Smith bought. He didn't fish it out of the water. He has a regular supplier."

"Who?"

"I don't know. Some entrepreneur—young Asian. I don't know if he works for someone or it's his own business. Every few weeks—I guess Smith puts in an order. A ship comes. Smith takes most of it—at least half—of what they bring."

Langhorn looked at me like a man uncomfortable with his

own inner quarrels. "It's more than he's pretending—or pretending by not saying—lets everyone assume he gets it all from the ocean; it's that the source of this *better* garbage.... I did a little research.... There are these horrible factories—operations—outdoor factories where all these cast-off—tons of it—plastic waste is...prepared. The poorest of the poor are working it, separating insulation from the metal in wires, melting things apart—black smoke of plastic fires. You know what burning plastic smells like." He actually looked distressed now. Although there were others not too far from us, I felt he and I were contained in this distressing vein which he was opening to me. I would not have thought the art critic one to worry about the struggles, the degradations of Earth's downtrodden, but apparently he was suffering from some sort of anguished epiphany.

"You've seen this? Yourself?"

He nodded. He looked full upon me. His face was sweating. Here and there, along the archipelago, in the distance, was the muted sound of machinery—the fact of Smith's "art" continuing, however Langhorn judged it. He said, "I'd read about it, seen some two minute film on one of the news magazines...but when I was in Asia— I wasn't just in Vietnam. I traveled. In China, especially. The pile of plastic debris in one of the operations I saw—talk about the apocalypse. The fires, the people working there—children, too. It was an image of hell."

"So Smith is making use of this hell."

For the first time he looked at me with the confidence of a man sure of his feelings and sure of the rightness of those feelings. "Yes, he is."

After a pause, he added, "That night, the storm, I was in the middle of a dream, the plastic hells, my little island tilted. It was tilting back and forth when I left. I didn't have some crazed breakdown of fear like Smith tells you—or infers. I just wanted to get away—a little."

"In the middle of—?"

"I wasn't going to sail across the Pacific. It was just the storm coincided with—these thoughts.... I was going back—"

"But going out into that storm—"

"I was confused. I got confused. I wasn't counting on a storm like that." He looked at me with genuine, vulnerable shame. He had meshed dreams and reality into some, well, useless action. "Then I ran into your ship. I wasn't—couldn't then—say exactly what was going on. I let myself sound a little crazed—well, I was feeling that way. Not because of a *storm*—"

I diverted him from his inner maelstrom. "How are you leaving here when you do? How did you get here?"

"On the ship that brings the plastic. That's how I came, that's how I'll leave."

"So you knew it from the beginning."

He looked away. "I did...well, not the extent. I just didn't put it together. But after the ship came several times...." He looked at the sweep of the plastic islands, at the visible evidence of his guilt.

I said, "So you're supposed to write about this—review it."

"Yes. Exactly my dilemma." He looked back to me. "I can just review it—and it's unusual enough, bold...but I'm also supposed to write about the vaguely environmental angle. Which, of course, is not my usual—"

He mentioned the magazine that would be paying him "very well" for both critique and narrative. I said, "So I guess you have the situation of whether to tell the truth or not."

He winced, slightly. "I hear you are a science writer."

"Yes."

"Would you—could you—see yourself—have you written about some scientific achievement but had moral concerns about it that you didn't write?"

"I guess so. Certain genetic engineering. Cloning. But if I privately question where it's all going, or is it moral in the first place, if I don't think I have a specific…well, evil, to point out, I don't have to say it."

His eyes grew large, studying me. "So then it's easier to ignore? If the big picture is wrong, but no one scientist *seems* to be committing a crime…."

I wasn't comfortable with this. "So Smith is committing a crime?"

"I'll ask you: is he?"

"I've heard Wal-Mart uses impoverished labor in other countries to make its products. It's like, I guess, doing business with companies who did business in South Africa when there was apartheid, or with Iran, North Korea, more recently." I persisted: "So: is Smith committing a crime?"

"He's certainly an accomplice to a social ill. And are you when you buy a product produced by Third World child labor?"

"Third World—?"

"They used to use that phrase a lot, not so much now. Not politically correct."

"I know what it means."

Langhorn said, "Not a crime—but an…evasion. Deception. Does the artist care about who makes his pigments? But he shouldn't pretend it's all from—this…." He made a defensive gesture to the vast ocean. The plastic islands receded in this vastness, the floating refuse smaller blips still.

I said, "He could make a case for using both sea garbage and the plastic from those plastic factories, as you called them—to bring them to light; and sell some of his weird creations and use the money to—"

Langhorn interrupted me. "He's committing the most common crime in human history: the crime of convenience. Consumers—and producers of products—will always adjust to convenience."

"So art is a product."

"Fulfills some want—some need...doesn't it?"

"You're the critic, you tell me."

He gave me a more enthusiastic smile suddenly, the smile of a man who has wholly confessed an inner quagmire. But he gave no reply, just a resigned grunt.

6.

A few hours later we were all back on *The Argus* with Hurston. He was saying, "I'm not sure if we should stay longer. It's all very interesting here, but we have to proceed. I don't mind staying another day—"

Melissa cut in: "Definitely one more day. I'd like to get some more footage." She looked at her watch. "I think there's something I'd like to get on film this afternoon." Blaise gave her an annoyed look that said, Oh, what was that?

Hurston gave the thought speech: "What?"

Melissa had that look of *I know something you don't know.* In the instant before she told us, I connected her earlier manner to my conversation with Langhorn—and *I* knew. She said, "There's going to be a ship arriving...." And she told us, if from a different viewpoint, about Smith purchasing plastic from some Asian dealer in tech refuse.

Hurston seemed genuinely surprised. "You mean all of this isn't from the ocean?"

Rory said, "I was beginning to think that. Looking at a lot of the plastic here—it looks like it hasn't touched the sea."

This was all perfect for the sardonicism of Rita. "The great ecological art project. Supplied by Asian sweat shops."

"I don't think it's that bad," said Melissa.

"I wouldn't be surprised if it is," Blaise let slip, letting show a bit of the fact that he was never Melissa's happy cameraman.

Without relating what Langhorn had told me, I said, "Those operations—scrap plastic, especially computers—most of them are pretty oppressive to the workers. Toxic. Just think of smoke from melting plastic."

Melissa was curt. "Whatever that situation is, I need to cap off this piece about Smith."

I wanted to pin her to something. "So he told you about this. How exactly did he explain it?"

"He didn't explain it, just gave me the facts."

"So he didn't think he was giving the appearance of being deceitful?"

The newswoman didn't answer right away. I think she was searching for an answer not so much to defend Smith, but to defend her own viewpoint. Her gemstone eyes glittered. "I think Arturo Smith would say...art only needs appearance— and we take that appearance and go somewhere with it."

"A non-answer," Rita said, bluntly.

Melissa snapped back, "You ask him, then."

Rita went from blunt to bland. "I will."

Hurston said slowly, "We'll stay for the ship—the rest of the day. We'll leave tomorrow morning. I find it disturbing, though. Definitely deceptive. I know about those tech trash operations. Hardly ecological." He said these last words glumly, with a hint of mocking efforts like his own, up against the ugliness of his species' bent to callous pollution.

Melissa's eyes appeared more mineral than flesh. "You're looking to me to pass a judgement. I report the news; the viewer judges."

Rita: "The judging always begins with what you report and how."

The newswoman was tense. "As straightforward as possible."

It was no surprise Rita at this point said, "If you were going to be so straight forward, you wouldn't've made your eyes so blue."

"And your breasts are natural."

This was definitely straying out of line. Rita spoke with stiff control. "They are. Should I strip so you can—?"

Melissa: "I'm sure there would be an audience who would love it."

Hurston cut in: "I don't think that's necessary, Rita."

Emile and Jorges, who had been in the background of all this, exchanged looks of amused disappointment. Not very different from the look that crossed Chapman's face, I thought.

Afterward I asked Rita if she really would have stripped. "In college I was an artist's model. I have no inhibitions about—"

"It's hardly an art class here."

"Don't think artists and students don't leer."

"I think it's a little different." Though I had to smile back at her laugh.

She gave a softer laugh. "It is different—I just wanted to confront her. I know she's not a *stupid* woman" (as if she were worse than stupid), "but something about her gets to me."

*　　*　　*

I could have—should have?—spent the following hours doing a bit more sightseeing of the archipelago of the plastic islands, but I stayed on aboard, and contemplating all this is solitude (as I often liked to do)—and found myself going through some stray notes I had written during our voyage: rather private and pithy (at least so I thought) observations about my crew mates. The confrontation between Rita and Melissa, the whole ambiance of our collective persona, now arrived at a very surreal setting (and the deception within that setting), pushed me to see if I still agreed with these recently written impressions.

*   *   *

When Melissa spoke about her past it hardly seemed reminiscences of the good and bad of growing up, of beginning—and succeeding at—her career, but the almost abrupt decision of a hungry mind that saw the need of self and made sure no contrary deed or influence would enter into her everyday. One could take that as a mark of artistic resolution, the decision of a special psyche that understood the nature of sacrifices needed to reach a goal; but to me it came across more like this: she saw the mask needed for a certain role—or believed a certain mask was required—and took that on absolutely. She didn't say, I want to be a famous—and unique—broadcaster, a face more eminent than the news, and bring an individual personality to that, she instead slipped into the costume of broadcast journalism's Central Casting: the trim, perky/serious attractive helmeted blonde, friendly and earnest to her viewers, an audience daily won by what amounted to a sham seduction. There had been no thought of another, truer, persona—say a brunette who looked back at the camera with a tinge of doubt about the facts that were being presented. She might have even gained the trump of a bit of sensuality for being outside the mold, not just a broadcaster.

Perhaps there was the rub. The hordes of women who had made it in the former Old Boys world had—been forced to?—

push an inherent allure aside to avoid charges of sleeping with the enemy, as it were. Oh, they were just about all attractive, these newswomen, but some sensual fire had been subsumed, even denied—for worldly success. Anyone protesting these thoughts could say: Do you want them to come on cooing like Marilyn Monroe for JFK? No. In essence, I want the mask removed. Male broadcasters were, in the main, hardly sex symbols, but it seemed to me they were what they were, while Melissa appeared only something she had forced herself to become. A decade ago she had been a minor player on a local station in the Midwest—now, almost the household name. The Faustian bargain—or is Faust here too profound, calling into the arena the fact of a soul to be damned? While Melissa had shunted that aspect of herself not to the devil, but like a dress to some inner clothing closet, as a garment that wouldn't do. So, not otherworldly bargain for worldly gain, but choice, a deed that would not bring madness and damnation in the end but simply the narrow, tight persona of a woman ever closed in the costume of her success.

All that being said, I had also thought she was far from the peak of the success she sought. What newscaster, whose animated portrait had been in five-days-a-week demand, could exit for a chunk of time to embark on the more than semi-quixotic mission of Hurston's? My guess about Melissa was that if she thought herself at the top she would not have budged from that spot; she believed she needed more, something to push her to a higher place. When I had asked about her almost open-ended commitment to Hurston's voyage, her reply was quick (like an answer long ago prepared?) and a little annoyed, as if I had perceived something she would rather no one recognize.

"I like to expand what I do."

That was it. True, false, or in between? A declaration simply part of the mask, the mask needing to be "recognized" for something that appeared *not* part of the costume? Or was this only another level of the costume? Her foothold more than gained at the networks, she devotes her persona to this encroaching plastic menace of the seas? So was it something of integrity trying to get out of the costume, or a further layer of that mundane psychic apparel? Watching her order Blaise around, a bitchy director of this enviro-drama, it was hard for me to believe in her sincerity—but: maybe it was not a case of either/or, but of an uncomfortable mix of both. Melissa Connors, one of the new queens of the TV news scene, troubled by a dichotomy, which she had surely believed wholly rooted out in childhood.

*   *   *

And the woman who "just wanted to confront her"—

The way I heard Rita explain it, her passion for the ocean was born of her parents' divorce—and the fact that they were of separate continents. Her mother was British, her father American. "Though," as Rita said, "his family could trace itself back to the 1700s—came from England before the Revolution. And illogically, being centuries removed from England, a lot of times they acted—some of the family did—as if America were a country they'd just come to, disapproving of the way things were done there."

With the divorce, Rita stayed with her mother in England most of the year and would come to America on long holidays and for most of the summer to stay with her father. She would find herself, at the age of ten or eleven or twelve or older on the shores of England or America (both parents lived near the ocean) wondering at the psychic—and physical qualities (not her words, mine)—of the great element that swept away before her, both separating and linking the two continents from which the very biological essence of her own creation had sprung. And that *was* more or less how she put it, adding some further bio-metaphysics: "Like this great womb I had edged out of, but was so close to, and I could *feel* its rhythms, its currents, like blood."

And don't they say blood is thicker than water?

She came to study the water-arteries of the planet, as if her feelings of separation and connection had given her a task, a duty; then, as happens in such matters, her discoveries brought her beyond the impetus that had taken her to their course in the first place.

"It was like a secret that I knew, how the oceans moved around the whole world. Of course, there were a lot of people who knew—but it was special in a certain way to me. This rhythm of the water, how the cold of the poles became the warmth of the equator or the other way around, how the cold and warm currents brought different temperatures to different coasts—this exchange, this change, of motion and temperature, the creatures that used it as roadways…the way *we* have, the way we are doing now: connected into an energy whose mechanics we can describe—but; how did it begin? It's like life itself. God, or Darwin, or some mix: why are the waters of Earth in *this* way? And then our not so subtle mechanics of how we're affecting all this—and maybe in ways that are beyond the obvious."

She gave me a smile, one of rueful self knowledge, of intimating that there were things that would take too long to explain. "Sometimes I think I hooked onto this—this adventure with our captain—to escape a greater explanation for the obvious. Plastic pollution: you can see it. Yes, it gets degraded into the minute, but for the most part we *see* our deed."

"No," I said, "I think you perfectly belong here." She cocked her head, on the verge of a laugh that was a question. I said, "You're riding the currents—to some center: of us and the Earth."

"Poetic," she announced, whether with appreciation or with her sardonicism I wasn't sure.

It came to me after this conversation that Rita's sardonic quality must have been born from that childhood, looking across the ocean of separation, discovering the secrets that others knew, and in this way knowing human beings worked their lives upon or alongside a primal vastness that mocked their posturing—or more precisely, was indifferent to it. And she knew her knowing was much less than the true knowing. Whether mapping the blood belt of the planet's currents, or noting how pollution was carried in its ugliness upon this blood, there was indeed something so vast at work here, she might even have to scorn the apparent desire of a Hurston, who was angry at the human defilements inflicted upon the world. Life itself, Nature itself, defiled its creatures, the billions upon billions of living things, born to quick death—whether in hours or a century. Against Time, all are nothing. The womb, the womb of that ocean that had separated her parents, the creation of her mother's egg and her father's sperm, the human womb from which she had come, gave only the short time for life's harshness and beauty—then, done. This was nothing profound I saw, and if I conclude Rita bore this in her manner, perhaps I might be the one who visions incorrectly. Though it was not an intellectual feeling, but a visceral one.

                              *   *   *

Reading these two assessments of personalities I wondered how much were of my own affectations. But they were definitely visceral, and so could not be, at least to me, untrue.

Perhaps I should add something about me....

As I said, I was born in 1984; yes: a millennial. My father

was a Black Panther back in the 1960s and '70s. As a young guy digging the hippie scene in New York, he and a friend, a white kid from Queens, hitched from the east coast to the west, arriving in San Francisco in the autumn following the so-called Summer of Love. My dad got involved in the newly formed Panthers across the Bay in Oakland. When he talked about those days, I saw his heart had fully plunged into the ethos of his time, the adventure and the passion. From the west coast he travelled to other cities, involved in different chapters of the Panthers, reconnected with his hitchhiking buddy in LA, then going with him to the wild convention in Chicago in 1968.

The influence and the idealism of the Panthers perhaps reached their peak at the very end of the '60s; by the '70s, insidious pressures and illegal tactics by the FBI, as well and inner failings of a number of the Panthers themselves, drove a paranoia through the movement; my father was accused of being unfaithful to the cause; he spent some time hiding out both from the American government and the Panthers themselves—aided by some Panthers, hunted by others.

I'm condensing a very long and more complex story. By the '80s the dust had settled. He met my mother, who had just graduated with a history degree. She was nine years younger than my father; when a girl, she had seen the Panthers as heroes. When she reached adulthood, the Panthers were really no more. My father was a hero of an era just completed—and already longed for? Anyway, they had me. My father would eventually become a professor of Black History; my mother, after raising me and my brother, went back to school and is now teaching a course she basically created: The Psychology of History—treating historical movements and events through the matrix of group and individual psychology: how did the Russian people create a Stalin? How did the American people create a slave economy?

I realize I am talking about my parents, not myself. I do this to show I grew up in an environment in which there was an intense *awareness* about things, intense opinions. This was certainly a special way to grow up. I am really grateful for it. At the same time, that awareness, those many opinions and perspective of my parents that I absorbed, formed in me my own awareness and opinion that human events ever rode on a train whose destination—and speed—was formed by passions, by the unconscious, as much as, if not more than concrete and logical ideals.

So I was drawn to science. (My analogy of the train recalls Einstein's explanations of relativity, using a passenger on a train and someone watching a train go by; the perspective of each of the same event is different—relative.) Not so much the doing of science, but, in a way like my parents, describing it. Though not dryly, I hope, not abstractly. Interwoven in the path of knowledge, of experiment, were human passions. As there were, here, on *The Argus*.

Added much later: As I looked over these notes again, I realize I was the perfect scribe for how this voyage would unfold.

Though I was not sure I would be satisfied with what I would draw from the odyssey.

7.

It was late in the afternoon when the dark ship grew on the horizon. Hurston passed the binoculars to me. I had already placed an ominous purpose on the vessel, so its dark, bulky appearance was translated in my emotions as indicating something more than a functional, industrial design. I felt, literally, an oppressive weight approaching us.

And then Hurston said the words I was, if not thinking, than feeling, in a distinct way. "There's evil in all this trash, isn't there?" He was staring at the ship, slightly squinting, as if trying to affix some detail. I said nothing. With gut instinct he was connecting trash and evil to the ship. He went back to studying its approach, raising binoculars to his face. With his eyes hidden by the bulk of these optics, he added, "We're so brilliant. We make more and more—then...."

Just down the deck from us Melissa was looking through her own binoculars, and directing Blaise to aim his video equipment seaward.

As the ship grew nearer and larger in size, I saw some of the workers paused in their isle-creating labors and look to the black vessel. I didn't read anything worried or ominous in their looks—just...was it resignation? And Smith, as the ship grew very close, was at the edge of Gilligan's Island, by his plastic dock, where apparently the ship would come right alongside *The Argus*.

It came, with writing from several Asian languages on its side and in fact flying the flag of several Asian countries. I thought a ship had to be registered in one country alone. I'd have to check on this. Smith's wave to the figures on deck was habitual and pleased.

I left the deck of *The Argus* and came up to Smith. I asked, "What's the ship's name?"

"Translated loosely, *The Gatherer*."

This was appropriate, I thought. Smith had voiced no explanation about the ship. He acted as if everyone from *The Argus* knew something of *The Gatherer*. But Smith knew nothing of my conversation with Langhorn; maybe he had assumed, correctly, that Melissa had told the rest of us.

Some sailors in shorts and T-shirts disembarked onto the plastic shore. There was a babble of languages. Then a dark haired man who was obviously in charge of things descended from *The Gatherer*. He looked in his mid thirties. In the heat of the Pacific summer he wore black pants and a black short sleeved shirt that flapped open to show a slim but muscular torso. Smith and the man bowed to each other, Smith smiling, as if happy to be in sync with this foreign custom. Then it was the turn of the custom of Smith's hemisphere: they shook hands. "Mr. Fukara," said Smith with formal, happy enunciation.

He introduced Louis Fukara to us, as if the latter and the crew of *The Argus* had been expecting each other. And as if, I thought, it did not matter to Smith that his appearance of using just plastic refuse from the Pacific was not the sole source of the substance of the islands. I was struck right then with the fact—which I had witnessed before and would again—that most people don't expect others to hold them to an absolutely pure standard. You move a bit in that direction (Smith *was* using debris from the ocean, after all), but you fall short of it—but you never say you do, and others still applaud you; or at least do not condemn you.

And it was obvious Fukara had had no wish—saw no need—to be covert. After greeting each of us (I could pick up no trace of an accent), giving Rita a lingering eye, and seeming pleased at Melissa's inquiries about being filmed (as Blaise was still working away, with his digital eye) he boomed out, to Smith, to all of us: "How are my islands!"

"Just look," said Smith, gesturing happily to the stretch of the archipelago.

Fukara said to us, "I deal in scrap—and Arturo makes art. Well, art is in his name." The two men laughed with each other, like two friends happy with a shared familiarity.

Smith said to us, "Louis came from where you sailed from—San Francisco."

Nodding and smiling Fukara said, "Yes, I grew up there." – As if this was a pleasure we must share with him.

So that's why the lack of accent. Then the language—or languages—he spoke to his crew in—had the accent?

Fukara was saying, "Though since I was twenty I've worked on the other side of the world."

"For profit or heritage?" asked Rita. It was typical remark from her. Smith gave her a look, divining something.

Louis Fukara only seemed pleased Rita had addressed him. "It seems to work out to be both. I am engaged to a Japanese woman and we have decided to raise our children Japanese, instead of American. Though I am sure they will speak both languages."

I noted that here was another engaged man giving Rita the assessing eye. I wondered if Rita played on this, and was amused at asserting her female powers. Did this make me envious—even jealous? Maybe a little. I admit I often considered myself too, well, plain. Occasionally I had thought about the transformation of cosmetic surgery—and just then I made the connection (perhaps because cosmetic surgery and these plastic islands had some sort of link): A woman's beauty is a treasure and what floated here was garbage.... But if you could make garbage into art, plainness into beauty—

Rita was saying, "So the future is in the Pacific?"

Fukara made a slight bow to her as he said, "Everyone has his own future. I think mine is."

I had to say—I couldn't help it: "You don't think Fukushima has made the Pacific a little—questionable?"

With quick self-certainty he said, "Oh, that's years ago now."

"Isn't it still leaking into the Pacific?"

"The Pacific is so big—one little accident in Japan— I won't say it wasn't serious—" He gestured, smiling. The smile was of a confidant man in the brightness of summer making transparent—and baseless—the fears of the mind's darker seasons.

Fukara added, "They're storing all that contaminated water in a thousand containers."

"And they plan to release it."

"I've heard several plans: let the water evaporate—"

"Leaving radioactive residue."

"More easily to dispose. Or dilute the water, bring it down to safe levels."

I didn't reply. Of course, I disagreed. We were indeed years past "the accident," but as far as I knew, along with the radioactive water that was contained, other radiation was still leeching from the plant into the ocean. Yes, the Pacific is huge, enormous—but just as one virus can take over a cell, proliferate and spread throughout the body…and be released into the water-arteries Rita so well knew—

In fact, I'd previously had a talk with Rory about how radiation might affect the plastic detritus of the Patch. He'd said, "That's one thing I'm really curious to know. Radiation doesn't just change the molecular structure of life, but the inanimate as well."

*   *   *

Neither Fukara nor Smith had any problem about us seeing just what *The Gatherer* had brought. Actually, there was no way to avoid seeing any of the new addition to the raw materials for Smith's art. It was tumbled out onto the plastic shoreline of Gilligan's Island, several irregular little hills, a separated mass whose plastic surface seemed to literally glitter in the sun in some places, did not glitter—or reflect—in others, and had, for me, a sort of intrinsic sadness: piles of ravaged things human beings had once used—and bought. The morass of plastic junk ran from the high tech (computer parts, etc.) to the very low tech: buckets of plastic spoons, forks and knives. There were also huge hairy balls of copper wiring. I mean huge: a number of semi-orderly, semi-tangled masses of wiring half as tall as a person—again, like the rest of this loot, both glittering and dull in the hot light. (Did I say "loot"? A Freudian slip?)

Smith seemed especially happy about the wire. "More than I expected," he said to Fukara. To us the artist said, "I intend to add a bit of copper to my work—some new ideas—metal on plastic—I'm visualizing a network—"

What Hurston said was deliberate and meant to pierce Smith's easy manner. "I hear it's a pretty toxic process, separating—melting off—the wire coating from the copper. There was something in *National Geographic*—"

Smith gave him a curious look, not unpleasant, as if Hurston had simply said something that was incongruous. Fukara's response was a little more defensive. "It takes expertise to do it correctly. And there's incentive to do it well." His smile of perfect white teeth was broad—and final. There was a Japanese stamp on it: to continue to discuss the matter would not be proper.

I was certain Rita did not care about such proprieties, but she was quiet. Hurston did continue, in a way. "The tech trash operations I'd heard about had been in Africa—" As if to absolve the Asian. Though Huston added, "But I know it's all over."

Fukara made the slightest bow; it seemed somewhat mocking. "Where there are resources—and money to be made—to be *extended*...." He straightened, smiling: as if he had just given the happiest explanation.

*   *   *

I drifted away from this. I wandered about the confines of the largest of the plastic islands; though you could hardly call it a large island. I noted from a distance the huge balls of wire being unwound, and some of it, along with various other plastic booty (yes: "loot" and "booty") that Fukara had brought, being ferried to other islands. I saw, amidst the archipelago, the incomplete ziggurat received a boat load of these supplies. The small figures on the shore of that isle appeared at this distance to be depersonalized beings, ordered either directly or through some ethereal osmosis by Smith, whose presence filled Gilligan's Island with loud happy talk which I could hear even at a distance. It seemed to me the deceptive jabbering of one who has to keep up a façade. It occurred to me that Langhorn wasn't around—not that his absence had any particular meaning— Or did it?

Rita joined me. She smiled as if she knew my thoughts. I said to her, "I expected you to get into a...debate with that— that dealer, should I say? He gave me the feeling he might as well be a drug dealer."

Rita laughed. "That's exactly it. Or actually, his true title is: Arturo Smith's patron."

I said, "Smith is more Fukara's patron. Smith buys."

"You're right. Drug dealer is closer." She squinted down the stretch of the archipelago. "How's ziggurat island?"

"I guess it'll be rising to its planned levels."

"Let's go over." At my look she said, "Smith doesn't act like anything's off limits to us. He's proud of every weird thing here."

"So you think it's weird."

"Oh, I think it's unusual. And it may even be art. But there's something bad involved in it."

"Fukara's supply."

"That's the obvious badness. Something also amiss psychically about it, I don't know."

There were many small boats, some powered, some simply rowboats alongside the island. And so Rita and I rowed out to the ziggurat. When we were just a hundred feet or so from Gilligan's Island, I saw Hurston suddenly sight what we were doing. He waved to us with sudden energy, I think he called out, but the loudness of some plastic rendering machine from somewhere drowned his voice. Rita and I shrugged at each other, and soon were at the ziggurat.

8.

It had been formed in an artful way, that was clear. The plastic levels—there were four of them—had been roughed and darkened, so from any distance they looked like stone. We walked along the base, tapped the plastic, almost like children pleased at the fact that something which appeared to be stone had the lighter texture of something like a giant toy. The several workers who had noted our arrival and who watched our playful inspection (but it wasn't playful, really) did not seem pleased we were there, but none of them said anything. I wondered which one—if any—was the creator of this project (what was the name Smith had told us?). But then we did meet him, directly on the other side of the ziggurat. A slim youngish man, who introduced himself sternly, in a heavy accent: Alfredo Santiago. Rita got the customary lingering look, even if it was of the slightest instant. It was like a man noticing a striking woman in a magazine then the next moment turning the page indifferently. I had the feeling Alfredo could not have repeated either of our names a minute later. I was not important to him at all, and even with the sudden distraction of Rita's body, there was the obviously feeling from Alfredo that he did not care much for distraction. He was solitary, artistic, caring very much about the work—his work—at hand, and begrudged any visitors—curious, approving, disapproving, whatever. Visitors were interruptions. The workers on the isle were merely laborers; like Arturo Smith, Alfredo was creator and director.

When Rita asked him, "What made you want to create a ziggurat?" he frowned, as if the query, the source and reason for his creation were unsatisfactory in themselves, and might force him to give an answer that could be nothing more than a disguise of words.

He was polite, if not friendly. He said: "Most people are more…drawn—yes, that's the word, to pyramids than ziggurats. But I find…the pyramid just goes straight up— the sides of a triangle. The ziggurat has levels. You are on one level, which is the base for the next level. Each level, the higher you go, is smaller than the one before it. One level created upon the other, smaller and smaller. You have the sense…that to ascend…is more concentrated." He raised his eyebrows at us as if that last word might be revelation to both him and us, adding, "And at each level is a space around the next level, between the edge of one level and the beginning of the higher level—like a resting place. A space to gather—something…" (he said this almost longingly) "before the next level."

Rita said, "But you climb the ziggurat with steps—that are really apart from the levels, not clamber over levels—"

Alfredo winced, as if this were a ridiculous point. "Yes, but the *sense* of it. Even if you don't *think* it as you ascend—it's there. And *in* the building at top…."

I said, "So it's the spiritual essence that draws you."

He looked proud and formal. "You could say that. At the top is the smallest space—"

"For the elect?" Rita broke in.

Alfredo frowned. "What does that mean—elect?"

Rita gave her sardonic smile. "It's a Christian term. Well, Protestant. Those better than the rest. Because God chose them. They didn't earn it."

Alfredo took that with an expression that said: *You are saying there is something I did not earn?* Aloud he said curtly, "I am not thinking of God."

"Just the works of man."

He didn't like that Rita was obviously toying with him. "We work how we have to. I can't judge what's beyond this."

I had to agree with him. It was Rita's turn to frown. There was a brief silence. Rita said, "How high is it going to be?"

"Two more levels."

We were interrupted when one of the workers, a middle aged woman—at least she looked it; she might have been younger— brown and squat with braided hair down her back, came up to Alfredo and shot off several sentences in Spanish. Alfredo said to us, "I have to get back to—"

"Of course," I said. "Thank you for your time."

Rita and I were left on one side of the ziggurat while Alfredo and his minion went around to the opposite side, out of sight. Rita said, "Ziggurats, chess pieces—a strange archipelago. Or is he really going to float this off the coast of…New York, San Francisco? He should make it a lighthouse at the top. That would fit into the spiritual—light at the zenith…."

At my twisted smile, actually more of a smirk, she said, "I'm just babbling."

"Mocking—like you do."

She sighed. "I'm obvious I guess."

I wasn't trying to be polite when I said, "We all are." It was an abrupt response that was my own (banal) revelation.

*   *   *

We saw another squat woman, short, appear from around the corner of the ziggurat, and who seemed to be vacuuming, the wire from her machine trailing some distance behind her. I suppose plastic that had been worked left plastic dust? It was another surreal sight of the plastic islands. I've seen hundreds of these woman before in the U.S., Latinos—Latinas—illegal or not, stolidly vacuuming public places: offices, schools, gyms; the new underclass cleaning up after those with more secure lives and better paying jobs. Or so it appeared. At a gym I frequented I had sympathized with the Hispanic woman— very short, like this one here—going about the different exercise equipment weaving her way among the slimmer, more apparently fit gym-goers, the vacuum on her back (in the manner of leaf blowers), and with a very long multicolored cord unwound behind her. Then one day I noted her in a corner, texting on the newest and most expensive phone. Perhaps her one luxury among a frugal, hard working life in a country foreign to her birth. Of course, even the poor today have these phones. But viscerally I felt the cell phone an indication of an iceberg tip that revealed the woman to be not as downtrodden as my earlier impression had her being. Feelings are things you can't prove in a court of law, but you don't deny then. At least to yourself. The workers I had seen on Smith's islands, many of them Hispanic, just like the landscapers, the fast food workers and so forth back home, were working for purposes I suddenly realized I had already decided: not for the glory of Smith's conceptual artwork, but because it was a job, well paying or no;

and perhaps they were as amused at the product of Smith's fancies, and thought their own duties nonsense if remunerative.

Of course, Emile and Jorges hardly shared Hurston's ecological vision, either. I had my own vision of a huge swath of humanity, that population descended from the conquered Indians and the conquering Spanish of hundreds of years ago infiltrating the direction and business and tasks of North America, not in agreement with any particular intent, but for food and shelter, a foothold that, once more firmly established, will take off in its own direction. There is nothing new in these thoughts; and yet I knew I would be—I was—working among the directions the coming Hispanic directive would displace. Or, to be more accurate, both sides could become different, very much other than what we thought ourselves to be. How appropriate—or ominous—that this woman vacuumed the ziggurat of the Mesoamerican culture Europeans subjugated, with hardly thought to centuries-old genocides, and any consideration of the future that otherwise would have come. What that future *would have been* no one can know, but odds are it would not have been this one, of Smith's plastic archipelago.

In the manner she had appeared, the woman disappeared around the next corner of the ziggurat, though the wire of many colors was still in sight, giving evidence of her presence and passage. I said nothing of my thoughts to Rita, or to anyone afterward.

It was only much later I wondered what that cord was plugged into.

9.

Soon we were back at Gilligan's Island. It seemed Arturo Smith was still sorting through the bounty of *The Gatherer*. A large portion of the plastic island was covered with the high tech debris, which had been spread out from its original piles. Smith moved about and within this, apparently with the pleasure, to use the cliché, of a kid in a candy store. Fukara followed, though in a more perfunctory business manner. Smith was seeing the materials for his strange art; Fukara was seeing money. I wondered if Smith had his choice of what to buy or not, and leave Fukara to return to the Orient with not very much for procuring and transporting this cargo. The fact that Smith was picking through this morass of castoff objects indicated this might be the case; but then, I could hardly imagine Fukara, who seemed the smooth businessman, taking a risk like that. I guessed that if Smith rejected any or all of what Fukara had brought, the Japanese still gained a fee. Perhaps it was a set fee plus what amount of booty Smith chose. Why I was so intent about thinking about this I don't know. Perhaps it was a "scientific" assessment of one part of the operations of the plastic archipelago.

I saw that Smith did eventually reject some of the debris—maybe a fifth. So you'd have to say Fukara had chosen well. His look was that of a man who had concluded a successful business deal as he gestured for his crew to take the rejected material back on board. –Where did that rejected garbage go? I wondered.

But then, one of the island's workers, one I hadn't noted before, hurried up to Smith and began gesturing toward the rejected materials. He was an odd looking man, with a homely face and thick tangled hair, stooped, a posture that gave the suggestion of a hump on his back, in clothes that were appreciably soiled. It was hard to access his age. He looked like something out of a fairy tale. From this distance I could not hear what he was saying, but it was apparent he wanted some of the rejected debris. Whether his appearance (you instantly felt sorry for him) or the logic of his request made Smith benevolent, I couldn't say, but quickly he was acquiescing and Fukara's men abandoned some of the plastic trash to the homely worker and some of his peers. I could not see any distinction in what this gnome-like man had chosen from Fukara's cargo, but then I suppose I did not have the special inner vision for what various tech trash could be.

A few minutes later, before going back onto *The Argus*, I bumped into Langhorn, who now seemed retreated to the fringes of all this conceptual art, of whose passion and essence he was supposed to write. When I mentioned the scene with the odd-looking worker ("Almost looks like he's hunchbacked—") Langhorn said, "That's Hugo. He was born a little deformed—"

"As in Victor Hugo, who wrote *The Hunchback of Notre Dame*?"

"Just coincidence, I think." Then he considered. "Though maybe—anyway: The story that Smith told me was that he was affected by some chemical pollution the Soviets had left behind in one of the republics they abused for the generations of their regime. But Hugo's got a peculiar talent, got a special eye for the sort of thing that Smith does: garbage into art."

"You say that with—sarcasm?"

Langhorn shrugged. "Smith discovered him—somewhere. Some back woods local fair in Eastern Europe, selling trash as art…crafts. He's done that before—always takes a little of what Smith rejects. As if—I think—he wants to show Smith he can make something out of things even the master sees as useless."

"And does he?"

"It's all subjective. He does make use of what he picks. Whether he matches—or exceeds—Smith is anyone's opinion."

"So what's your opinion?"

Langhorn sighed. He looked past me a moment, into the distance, the activity of the island. "I suppose I'm rethinking all of this. As I said. Or did I say exactly that?"

"You were having...moral doubts."

"Moral?"

"As to the source—of Smith's—"

Langhorn laughed, a little self mockingly. "A critic having moral doubts. Scandalous. Dereliction of duty."

"Perhaps morality is the highest form of criticism."

"That's too witty for me to counter."

"It wasn't meant to be witty."

"Profound, then."

Langhorn returned to *The Argus* with me. It was plain he felt more comfortable with Hurston's crew than Smith's. And Hurston was engaged in something that would perhaps make the choice even more pronounced.

It seemed that it was unconscious purpose of each of us to gather in Hurston's cabin; and, it seemed, he had unconsciously expected it.

To the surprise of all of us, he had the internet up on his laptop. The laptop used by both Hurston and Rita was recharged by the ship's solar powered generator, but the internet had not been accessed since we'd left San Francisco.

Hurston pointed a small rectangle sticking out of his computer. "My Net Stick. It doesn't work all the time, but enough. Pulls in the satellite.'"

"Would that work on my laptop?" asked Rita.

"Probably."

"And you've been keeping it for yourself."

Hurston paused then gave a sort of *mea culpa*. "I guess I should have told everybody. But look—I want to show all of you— I've read about it, and there are plenty of photos and videos—about how all this high tech trash is processed. What I've got here is from Africa, though it's a lot in Asia, too."

The laptop's screen filled with a vivid photograph of an African woman. If she was poor her clothes were colorful—a vivid dress, with a multicolored cloth wrapped around her head. She needed that headgear, because as in those photographs everyone has seen of African women carrying bundles or great jars of water on their heads, expertly balanced, this woman bore a weight: of twisted wires—an enormous ball of copper stripped of its plastic coating. A woman with a head of copper snakes. Her face was in profile, a dark pensive face, looking immemorial, inured to toil, to the unfair demands of life; in her eyes was the sort of spirit that was beyond the tiredness and burdens her flesh had to suffer. For she was in the midst—or on the edge of—a definite hell. In the background were small blurred figures, masses of debris, and from one conglomeration of trash a thick, billowing smoke rose and spread—against a sky that was a grey, rough curtain because it had been veiled by the vile practices of earth. Imagination struck me with the taste of that smoke in my throat; I gulped and coughed at the toxic thickness.

In silence we looked at the photo for a while. We might have been stilled before a work of art. Then Hurston coughed—did he gag, too?—and clicked on a video.

A boy, fourteen or fifteen, thin, with bony shoulder blades, darted among small fires. He was melting the coating off the wires that the Hydra-headed woman would carry. A British voice narrated the sad story of the boy, whose name I didn't catch (anyway, he was more representative than individual), the pittance he earned from this toxic labor, and translated when the youth, facing the camera, said, "There is always a time in the smoke when I can't breathe. I choke. And it stays in me." The boy had a large head (all the more prominent for his gauntness), large eyes, whose whites were the moats from which his dark pupils apprehended his labor, not asking for pity, it seemed, though of some other expression than resignation: eyes just stating the flavor of this hell he had to taste. Then there was a close-up of his hand, scarred from the burns of the many fires he had tended. Then a shot of him racing about the small labyrinth of the fires, but shot from a different angle, as if the cameraman retreated from before the boy with perfect synchronicity. He leaped through this hell and gave its vision, while he kept making way—while you felt in fact you were backing into this hell. For a moment the boy was less vulnerable than the viewer; at least he could see what was about—

"Great camera work," said Blaise, quietly.

His few words and the look on his face had something quite different from the manner he had projected before. Maybe he had more in him than being Melissa's begrudging eye, putting in his time while climbing the ladder to—something.

The video continued. We saw a family trudging away from one of these operations, mother, father, two children—boy and girl—carrying various items. The father had slung something indistinguishable over his shoulder; the mother and children carried buckets. Around them were wreaths of the toxic smoke—as if they were emerging from hell, but still claimed by it.

"That's enough for me for today," said Hurston, pushing himself away from the laptop—but leaving its lurid material still displayed.

It seemed enough for most of us, except Melissa who took over Hurston's computer and continued to go through the images in a quiet, intense manner. I couldn't be sure if she were simply gathering facts for her own purposes or emotionally touched by what she had seen.

*   *   *

I went on deck, into the hot light. I had an empathetic foul taste in my throat. The toxins that are forced on us....

As a young reporter, I did innumerable sidebar stories about the BP "spill" of 2010. In my irregular passage along the Gulf Coast as the warm spring turned into hot summer, I attended public meetings at which officials, who could handle guilt without it spearing themselves, sweated before righteous crowds—crowds often a little too self righteous. I sat in a fisherman's shack listening to a fifty-year-old fat man talk about the beauty of the fishing life that had been violated. He was black and I had the feeling he felt our shared racial heritage made me sympathetic to his situation in the way a white person could not be. Meanwhile I envisioned countless glistening fish brought up to the suffocating air. I observed the chain gangs of beach remediation collect tar from the sands—and once saw an actual chain gang of inmates do this, the prisoners' faces— black, white, brown—stolid or resentful at having to clean up the problems some rich corporation had caused. And, most tellingly, I saw the ravaged wildlife, birds and fish covered in oil, suffering with incomprehension this drastic, brutal change in their world.

Once, watching a young woman—possibly even younger than I was then—dousing a dazed, sometimes compliant, sometimes struggling pelican with detergent and water, the girl explaining to me that this simplest way was the best ("It breaks up the oil. You just wash it off—"), I asked her to estimate how many creatures won't get treated. She replied so flatly (she might have been saying, "It's rainy today"),

"How many people in Hell?"

Of course, the human denizens of the Gulf Coast, who in large part thrived on killing the marine life—for food, of course—consigned British Petroleum, the moment's Satan, to Hell. This was the sentiment of frequent graffiti I saw everywhere, simple declarations of BP YOU RUINED OUR LIVES, to the semi-illiterate murals with Grim Reapers and gravestones, the reaper's sickle often bearing the drear two letters, "BP." That fat fisherman, who sweated as much as those hounded officials at public meetings, though it was the sweat of one feeling no guilt, had said to me, "There are forty-nine states, and then there's Louisiana." Oh, he was a proclaimer for a way of life, a life so ripped apart by the callous application of an oil company's pursuit for product; while he, the fisherman, sweated with—as I saw it—his own sort of guilt, which he could not recognize, and mislabeled as anguish.

It did become, for me, a question of guilt. And the crowds at the public meetings did indulge in self-righteousness. Let he who is without sin…. But where were the Americans who had pushed their country to renounce itself from the yoke of oil this past generation? God, here were a plethora of angry citizens, some certainly born before the Arab oil crisis of the 1970s, some after, but everyone, everyone had spent so many years living with the mad knowledge that lives, *their* lives were beholden to the oil cabal; and many of the self-righteous had themselves worked on one of the hundreds—thousands—of rigs out in the Gulf—still out there. It was just that *this* one had failed, had brought disaster, catastrophe, the prelude to apocalypse. I thought that many of the hands raised, demanding to be heard, shouting to hell with parliamentary procedure, would not look at any of their guilt, as bystanders or even participators. WWII Germans complaining about the Nazis. That's hyperbole, maybe, but the whole morass that had sprung into the summer of 2010 became a transparent journey through human vanity and self deception—without hardly any promise of change in the future, whether the distant future or tomorrow.

I even had the feeling that, when BP's attempt to cap the well looked like it was finally succeeding, in midsummer, the aggrieved residents of this coast harbored some unvoiced and unadmitted-to disappointment that the travesty could not go on and give further justification to their righteous lamentations. Freud insisted we had a death wish, and I believe we have the stifling quality of wanting to express how wretched someone else has made our lives, how something outside ourselves befouls our every move. An avoidance, a transference to free us from the guilt. Or at least to hide it—from ourselves.

One day that August, I walked on a beach that two weeks before had been dotted with tar balls, and the shoreline streaked here and there with irregular lines of crude. There were still scattered remediations going on, workers in bright vests and hats, and, hovering about the level of sensory awareness, the scent of the crude. One sensed this place was still wounded. Would recovery bring full health? Or be stymied by some other human disaster?

I had looked beyond all this: to the sky above, the horizon, seeing *there* some purity we would not touch. But then, in two different areas, the dark spots of airplanes on their passage, worked across my eyes. We enter every realm. We are beyond the Earth now; I suppose we'll reach the stars. What will our minds and hearts be shaped like then? I wondered. Will we be fat, bitching fishermen, arrogant corporate clones, or—or what? "How many people in Hell?" the animal rescuer had said. Hell, of course, being immaterial, can accommodate exponential hordes. Ironic that we invented this nonmaterial realm to recognize we are guilty, but have so much difficulty grasping the guilt *here*, where it most needs to be recognized.

10.

The next morning we left Gilligan's Island and the archipelago. Smith saw us off with great friendliness. Hurston was cool. Either Smith did not catch this, or, if he did, ignored it. Fukara and *The Gatherer* were still there—though I expected the remnant of that cargo of demonically obtained tech trash would be returning to wherever soon. The Japanese merchant was just as cool and polite as Hurston.

Hurston had asked Langhorn—I had, too—if he wanted to come with us. "You've probably got enough for your article," said Hurston.

Langhorn's reply had been a resigned one. "Enough, yes. But to do it correctly—as I see I should do it—I have to stay. Not long. I'll be picked up in another nine, ten days."

I had asked Langhorn if he were going to write about the "social aspect" (yes, I put it euphemistically) behind the source of Smith's artistic materials. Langhorn had made a long, low "Hmm…." Then he said, "A sidebar."

"So you will say something."

He had spread his arm outward, like a wave of surrender. "I will have to."

"I don't think Smith will be pleased."

"Critics are not supposed to please artists."

"But you'll be questioning his morals, not his art."

Langhorn had looked at me with an expression that had recalled Rita. "Do people believe they have to defend their morals anymore?"

We had exchanged emails. My first not so favorable

impression of the critic had changed. He was in the position of a man who might still lie about things to his public, but in private he would know them as lies; so I could appreciate this in him. Although my own field of writing appeared very different, there were lies in the scientific community as well—theories that became declarations of fact and brought their proponents kudos on the scientific and even the public talk circuit, with any tainted, conflicting facts within their research studiously ignored. Perhaps all of human life requires some self deception, and it's hard to know where the line is crossed into a sort of intentional malevolence. Certainly after hearing about—and seeing—the nature of the majority of the source of Smith's materials, that line had been left far behind.

At any rate, I don't think any of us, including Melissa, regretted leaving the plastic islands behind. Though it was a slow farewell. We had to sail along one stretch of the archipelago, past a scattering of complete and incomplete islets: the knight chess pieces, something like a city skyline á la Dali, a number of abstract creations, and, yes, the ziggurat, which had increased to another level. Some of the workers stopped in their labors and watched us pass, a true motley crew of artistic toilers who had somehow become bound to Smith's vision. People of various cultures, ages, races—you might have called Smith an equal opportunity employer. Some of those workers appeared to study us for a long time—as if we were leaving with some kind of message from them, some kind of...hope? A fantastical thought, but I had it. Some glanced for a few seconds then turned away. We were strangers in their universe, not to be too long regarded. By the ziggurat Alfredo surprised me by waving to us, a much friendlier gesture than any he had given Rita and me when we had visited. It was probably the friendliness of relief, I decided. We had no further chance to be prying—and asking "spiritual" questions about his creation. Rita in fact come up alongside me as we passed the ziggurat, and gave Alfredo a wave in return—friendly or sarcastic, I wasn't sure, for she did say to me, "That was some sideshow."

I wasn't sure if she was referring to the ziggurat or the entire archipelago. I replied with equal ambiguity: "As striking as the Great Pacific Garbage Patch itself." Rita tilted her head, gave me a careful look. I immediately thought I'd sounded pompous, but amended myself with only an enigmatic smile.

*   *   *

Emile and Jorges seemed more than relieved to be leaving the plastic islands. As I watched them renew their duties on *The Argus* I made the connection between them and the woman I had seen vacuuming the ziggurat—though they certainly seemed less oppressed (if that's the word) by the jobs through which they earned their bread in working for foreign masters.

I think both Emile and Jorges regarded me as not quite part of the crew—which, being a journalist (sorry, that word sounds too august to me, sometimes), I wasn't; but there was also the fact of my race and the rest of Hurston's gathered minds being white. So Emile and Jorges, if seeing themselves apart from them, perceived me as also being apart from Hurston's crowd—as I was also apart from the world of Emile and Jorges. It's hard for many to navigate life without these divisions.

As I had with Rita and Melissa, I had written some notes about Emile and Jorges. A little while after the plastic islands were out of sight, I reread them:

I cannot say Emile and Jorges are eloquent, but then I could not be understood in a language other than my native tongue, let alone use it adequately enough in the course of work. Could I go into some foreign country, brave the border crossing

(Hurston had inferred both were illegal) and find steady employ? Then again, America was this kind of place—both Democrats and Republicans needed someone to mow their lawns; and the nouveau riche of the Hamptons needed someone to tend their yachts tethered at the Westhampton Bath and Tennis Club and Marina, the docks at Sag Harbor, or Three Mile Harbor in East Hampton.

Not that I think they are deep men prevented from communicating profundities because of their failing at the weaker part of their bilingual universe. They are the salt of the Earth of any country: men who did the menial tasks better positioned men—and women—wanted them to do; and both Emile and Jorges understand this equation with an acceptance—and a little pride?—that they are necessary. The difference of course is that others might think—did think—the way in which they executed their particular skill (whether lawyer, CEO or, say, science writer) was special to them alone. There were others in their profession, yes, but each man and woman in such professions did not have to be a duplicate of one another. While with Emile and Jorges they knew they did things, performed tasks that could be easily performed by others; and that they were willing to accept this station. Oh, there were levels in their menial world, from landscapers to tending yachts—there was more than lateral movement there; but the role was the same. In the most casual conversation with them, I wondered if they perceived the future (other than the occasionally mentioned fantasy of winning the lottery) of perhaps owning a yacht themselves—and hiring other south of the border laborers to work for them?

But perhaps they were the truest of menials: expecting no possibility beyond the work at hand, glad only for its presence and whatever perks it might offer.

And then I wondered: if Emile and Jorges had been born in the U.S., and those Hamptonites they had served had been born in other countries, would the situations be reversed? I'm not politically correct, but intuition and experience has taught me that one's circumstance—family, money, country, etc.—had a lot to do with one's end point. Or, at least, the middle passage.

*   *   *

Later that day, reflecting on these notes as I again watched Emile and Jorges, I thought my words had both truth and a bit of hubris. Yes, *I* was the one who saw things clearly.... But that's all we have, here: our own visions. Experience and the self honesty to recognize what experience reveals—and how it might ravage an earlier prejudice. So we go on, with our words.

11.

As if in connection to my words to Rita, the Patch offered us other striking things.

With Smith's archipelago out of sight we were all once again paying attention—at least half attention—to the debris that bobbed on the surface; and among that debris, we saw the mannequin.

It was a brown mannequin, a brown female mannequin, the color of the race whose clothes it had been created to display, with two bumps for breasts, with one hand missing (the right hand) and part of the left leg missing from the knee down (as if that absence made a fact of symmetry with the absent hand). The rest of the mannequin was intact but weathered, the brown of the "flesh" faintly caked by the sun. The face, partly veiled by a strip of a fishing net, looked up at that sun, unblinking, its immediate thoughtlessness considering a universe apart from the natural world. Or had it been a white mannequin browned by exposure—a sort of plastic tan? When it rose slightly with the swell of the sea, I saw the green that emerged from below the waterline. Like the moon, the mannequin had its light and darker side: the brown bleached lighter, its back greened by the sea.

"Oh, my God," Blaise exclaimed. "For a second I thought it was a body."

As the simulacrum came right up alongside the ship and softly bumped against the hull, I heard Hurston say, "Should we take it?" He appeared surprised when Rory quickly and distinctly said, "Yes." Actually, it seemed Hurston had been talking to himself, and that it was himself alone who should answer. He gave Rory a look as if the latter had intruded upon a private choice. Then Rita said, "Of course." Outvoted (then again, he had not voiced a choice either way), Hurston did not wait for further tally. Emile, who seemed to be containing a laugh, threw a net over the mannequin, and it was hauled up.

Taken from its watery life, the mannequin had an even more unpleasant aspect. Its human form, its loss of half a limb (like an amputation), that partly veiled face that was meant to have no expression—it was all disconcerting. When it was lying before him, its wetness gleaming in the sun, it was plain Hurston wasn't happy to have it on board. Blaise seemed even more affected, "God, why do you want *that*?" he asked Rory, and might have said the same to Melissa, who now directed the mannequin to be filmed, and who even asked Hurston if we could throw it back into the water so she—via Blaise—could capture it being raised up, as if for the first time. Truth in media. I'd heard of presidents exiting Air Force One with the camera focused on them as they waved to apparent crowds though in reality there were no crowds; and I'd always considered that out and out deception. At least tawdry Melissa made her demands without shame and as if they were perfectly natural, even desirable, and she even gave a look to Emile and Jorges, as if anticipating Hurston's command to follow her wish. But our captain looked back at the newswoman with such annoyance—scorn might be the better word—that his single, succinct uttered "No" wasn't really necessary.

She sulked away and had to be content with Blaise recording Rory bending over the corpse-like mannequin with a magnifying glass, an odd Sherlock Holmes, studying the victim of a crime.

"She hasn't been at sea for *that* long," Rory pronounced, more to himself than anyone.

"*She?*" said Rita.

Rory looked at her, in this moment surprised at her usual sarcasm. "Well, it's obviously supposed to…*represent*—"

Rita's laugh freed him from further words. He threw a profanity at her. She laughed again, and happily glanced at Hurston when he said to Rory, "What are you going to do? Dissect it? Autopsy?"

Rory stood up to his long height, annoyed. His scientific rigor was being mocked. "This is plastic debris. You are all reacting—very primitively—by the…shape."

Rita shot back: "You're the one who called it 'she'."

Rory looked at me. "What's your scientific view?"

"I'm a little spooked by it. Just look at the eyes."

I had been looking at the mannequin's eyes since it had been brought on deck. The veil of the fish net had fallen back from the face. There were no pupils, yet…like those old statues of antiquity whose pupil-less eyes seemed to be seeing, to me this 21st mannequin had a disturbing gaze. Definitely *some* kind of gaze—

"There are no *eyes*," said Rory with exasperation. "I thought at least you would see this rationally."

I winced at Rory's comment, not at Rita's barking laugh. "Is that enough?" said Blaise to Melissa, who nodded, oddly distracted now, it appeared. Perhaps she too had noticed something in the eyes.... While Emile and Jorges stood a little apart from the rest of us, amused, I was sure, at this bit of discord a simple sea-weathered mannequin had caused.

The brown flesh had given me the thought: Unlike those pale mannequins that proliferate in stores, if interrupted more now by darker ones, this mannequin was supposed to represent a skin other than whiteness; but now it seemed more to me just a darkened white mannequin, not representing any of the races that had spread out from continents other than Europe. Of course, it's repeatedly said of black and brown people that they have "white features." I rubbed my eyes with one hand, as if trying to fix the true racial aspect—the intent—of this castoff form. Race continues to prick at us, and we fix our disguises of it (and our excuses) at different points along a line of perspective we are held at by both prejudice and experience, the former hopefully altered by the latter.

They must have been further amused later that day. Rory had been left to do what he would with this representation of a female. Then he had left it out there, on the deck. And Rita, ever mocking Rita, took it and lashed it to the bow of the ship, like a captive, grotesque figurehead, the pupil-less eyes directed at the destination of our odyssey, the shard of the now dried fishing net hanging to the side of the face, like an abstract representation of hair.

Rita apparently enjoyed Hurston's rage and harangue when he discovered it. "That looks sick!" was about the politest thing he said. Then, with the aid of her sarcasm—and her seductiveness—she actually won him over with a diplomacy and a rhetoric that showed how well she understood human nature. (Which was probably why she was forever sarcastic. If the passions of others appear so plain, they have to seem ridiculous to that discerning eye.) She told Hurston that the brown and bleached mannequin was the appropriate if macabre symbol for the Great Pacific Garbage Patch, for what human beings were doing to these waters. "Something you can't turn away from—not like a plastic hair or a computer part. Almost as bad as the children burning the plastic from wires—" And furthermore. Hurston finally laughed—in appreciation, in resignation. For there was truth to Rita's argument, truth to the appropriate irony in this unpleasant, degrading symbol. He surrendered his protest, resigned, at least for the moment, to this bizarre symbol of his quest.

Speaking of degrading, not just literally but figuratively, I did not disagree when Melissa said (as Blaise filmed the lashed mannequin), "It's sort of degrading to women."

Hurston, won over to the side of the symbol, said, "There are male mannequins. We just happened on this one. There's probably a Ken to this Barbie somewhere in the Patch."

Rita, being Rita as ever, said, "Maybe not. You know certain cultures like to kill off the female. This Barbie's Ken is probably in some shop window, nicely dressed."

"Or on one of Smith's plastic islands," said Blaise, who himself was being more openly sarcastic now, as if the longer he was out to sea with his mistress of the media, the more he felt a bit freer of the restraints of his ladder climbing.

That very evening he and I watched the sunset together, that great distant star of life settling redly into the west from which we had come, and the cameraman suddenly said, to my surprise, "Red sky at night, sailors delight—"

It just didn't seem like something he would say. "Where'd

you hear that?"

He shrugged. "Who knows?"

We drifted into a friendly conversation. It seemed he had left his edgy snippiness somewhere in the west.

He told me a little bit about himself. Growing up a young gay man in a small town in the Midwest, if he knew he (to use the oft-felt credo) "didn't fit in," at least he had not had to suffer through what previous generations of gay people had suffered. He knew in the world just beyond his immediate environs there were other places and opportunities. He'd been a TV junkie since a toddler, and had seen in that high definition rectangled world all the fantasies and reality he could want. Coming of age had meant coming to L.A. and New York, and being accepted in that medium—and media—no matter the eros he desired. "Though," he added, "sometimes I think it's gotten to the point that someone, *because* he's gay, thinks he's entitled…."

I smiled. "Casting aspersion on the newcomers."

His smile back was accepting. "I guess all of us—and I don't mean just gays—feel threatened if we haven't quite made it and feel someone at our backs."

I said, as if in diversion, but it felt pertinent: "Do you like Melissa?"

He laughed. "She's got her own climb. Not that she hasn't made it. I guess I don't seem to like her, do I? Do you?"

"She's of a type. As I had expected."

"That's diplomatic. I was saying: sometimes I think I came at just the right time. You don't have to be in the closet like in the past, and you don't have to be…*entertaining* because you're gay." Then he gave me a wry look: "Or am I being too cliché?"

I didn't have to answer; that was when we saw the first of the Buddhas.

Dark and with a fake patina, the plastic lotus-sitting Buddha was fairly close before Blaise and I spotted it, just when we'd turned from the glory of the sunset and beheld the bobbing icon.

"Is that what I think it is?" Blaise's voice was startled, and laughing.

We stared, as surprised as when we'd seen the mannequin, as the Buddha floated toward us, its head slowly rocking back and forth; it gently knocked against the ship. That tactile contact seemed the abrupt cue for the others we then spotted a floating half dozen or so, emerging in the twilight, all cross-legged Buddhas with variations—some with palms facing out, at shoulder level; with palms on lap; with beaded acorn-shaped headdresses; some slim others not; and each a different size. They jostled against each other and headed in the path of the first Buddha—so that when both Blaise and I raised the cry and the others came on deck, it was easy to retrieve these very strange apparitions from the sea as twilight become more rich and livid. They were netted like fish. Rita laughed as she extricated them from the net's webbing. Rory echoed with his own laugh: "My God, the gods are invading us," he proclaimed with ironic pleasure as he raised one wet Buddha up from the deck, its face and his on the same level, the Buddha with raised hands, palms forward. Soon all of us in the deepened twilight stood with the retrieved Buddhas—and Rita's laugh rang out again.

But there were still more Buddhas at sea. In the dimming we saw them, scattered and clustered. Hurston let out: "This is insane!" Rory, who had put down "his" Buddha, looked out on the various shapes and exclaimed a sound that was like a wordless happiness, followed by a laugh that was almost like Rita's. "Some temple out there must've gone out of business!" While Melissa, overstepping Hurston's authority, was yelling at Emile and Jorges to get some light on the sea, so she could have her trusty Blaise make this part of the visual record. I caught Hurston about to say something, but he apparently abruptly decided he didn't care—and was perhaps (as a sort of detached observer) curious to see how Emile and Jorges reacted to the newswomen's orders. They acquiesced. But not, I thought, because they recognized or granted Melissa any authority, but out of their own curiosity—and, I think, a little fear. I caught something in their faces. They had taken in most of the sights and incidents of this voyage with the perfunctory alacrity of laborers while tending to their duties. The purposes of Hurston—and even the rest of us—were strange, even inscrutable; and, ultimately, not to be regarded with much attention. But now, faced with this invasion of the plastic Buddhas, the Central American pair might be taking this for some kind of omen, if a metaphysic of a culture foreign to their own, a tipping point at least, that had pushed the inscrutable into, as Hutson had burst out, the "insane!"

Anyway, the searchlight they directed cut back and forth across the waters, side to side, all about the ship, and the floating Buddhas it illumined were innumerable. Rita and Rory netted more of them, brought them onto the deck; and then Emile and Jorges were doing the same. Reluctantly? I wasn't sure. Or as if they could break any power of these omens by bringing them close, and out of the subliminal power of the waters.

Then Hurston asserted his authority. "My God! That's enough!" He tore one of the Buddhas from Emile's hands and hurled it back onto the lapping surface of the newly night-doused sea streaked with searchlights. There was a little light left in the west, and the silhouette of some very brief cloud. Overhead, I saw a brighter star or two. It was with this glance upward I heard Hurston immediately alongside me command: "No more! Let them float over to Smith!"

His exasperation—his anger—stilled everyone, and there was this odd tableau, held for a long moment: all of us, on deck, the light swinging out over the sea and its masses of marine Buddhas. Rory, as if in ironic obeisance, tossed a Buddha he'd just worked out of the net back out to the darkening ocean. It made the faintest sound and slipped by the hull of *The Argus*, invisible now, proceeding to no destination at all.

*   *   *

Afterward, below, I said to Rita, "That was even stranger than Smith's islands. Makes you wonder: where they all came from."

I would have expected Rita to make some amusing sarcasm. But she made a face I couldn't read, a grunting sound, and just said, almost with a palpable weariness, "I'm for bed."

There was a glimmer here of something one hardly saw with Rita: a normal tiredness within the armor of her quick tongue.

But I didn't want to let her go without adding, "The mannequin, Buddhas—what next? Crucifixes?"

She just shook her head at me, smiling.

I went back up on deck. The summer constellations were bright above *The Argus* and reached, with equal brilliance, down to the horizon, the skein of the Milky Way diaphanous and profound. Though there was a contrasting light on deck that drowned out some of the stars. Not the searchlight; that was off now, just a small deck light that showed some of the Buddhas plainly, others in dark outline, and which did not really delineate the female mannequin lashed to the bow of the ship. In the midst of all this stood Hurston, hardly an Ahab, but clearly someone who had been confounded by the recent events of a voyage that had become much more than an environmental exploration of the Great Pacific Garbage Patch.

There was something very moody and alone about his figure.

He turned to me, a little annoyed, it seemed, that his intense solitude had been spied upon and blurted out, "I'll be glad when we get to the center, where everything'll be broken down—microscopic!"

12.

It was late in the day and four of us—myself, Melissa, Blaise and Rory—were watching the sun lower to the horizon. Apropos of nothing (boredom, perhaps), I asked Melissa what was "the most interesting thing you've ever covered—aside from this voyage?"

Melissa—and Blaise too, it seemed—looked back at me with what might have been a slight confusion, a shuffling of memories: the banal, everyday progress of shifting through the past and simultaneously deciding whether to answer the question honestly. After a pause Melissa, her face burnished in the sun's more horizontal light, blinked, as if apprehending a signal from an inner oracle, and said, "Hurricane Harvey: Houston underwater." Blaise gave a smirk and half nod. Melissa looked at him with a distant, vague smile and said, "The first time Blaise and I worked together."

Blaise grunted. "An auspicious start." He seemed about to add something else, but he gave what I can only call an uneasy glance downward, and said nothing more, as if he had seen a caution signaled to him from his better (but earth-hugging) angel.

There was a soft chuckle from Melissa. "We got there when the worst of the storm, the rain was over; it was still raining, but it just seemed a normal heavy rain, not the torrent it'd been. Of course, the flooding was not normal: *that* was apocalyptic.

I saw an overpass across a highway—how high are they? Ten, twelve, feet? A stretch of highway completely underwater, just the very top of the overpass visible. I think that jolted me, more than the human distress."

"Really?" said Rory.

Melissa raised her eyebrows. "Sarcasm?"

Rory smiled. "I'm not sure."

Melissa sighed. "I know some of you have the impression I just care about the story, not the people—"

Blaise: "I plead no comment."

"Blaise, why do I tolerate you?"

"Because you know I can tolerate you."

Melissa laughed. "What was I saying? OK, you see floods, people pulled out of houses—all that tragedy. And the absurd...that sort of drowns out (no pun intended) the tragedy. Like that very fat guy I saw slip out of the grip of his rescuers, flip right over into the water that was like a stream on this street, bob and float because he was so fat, but he was yelling like he was drowning. They got him back in the boat.

"But there was a lot more of the absurd than that. I saw all of the things you saw on the news; and then there were things you didn't. And those were the ones..." She hesitated—as if embarrassed? No, it was something else. She shook her head. "Well, bizarre weather, so there had to be a few bizarre things." She went on quickly. "We were with these rescue guys, four of them, in a boat, the streets were literally rivers. Got a lot of footage." She gave a diplomatic nod to Blaise. "It was the end of the day. Three of them we dropped them off at a firehouse that was standing just out of the water, like something in a dream, with the rain still falling. Though some part of the sky was getting lighter, like there was a sunset somewhere that wanted to get through. But the clouds stayed, the rain kept on.

"So we kept going around on this boat with this one guy. He was middle aged, heavy, he had sandy thin hair...and was determined, I guess, to be a rescuing angel. There's a certain psychology to people like that—that's another story. He said there was another block he wanted to check. He might as well have said another branch of the river, the way things were. I told him we'd film until dark. I was pretty beat by then."

Blaise: "You mean you'd have me film until whenever."

Another smile from Melissa, one I actually thought of as friendly. "Your first time with me. I thought I was giving you a lot of great footage."

"The thing about this business," said Blaise, "and I knew it long before I went to Harvey, whatever great footage I got, it'd be associated with you, not me."

"I can't argue with that. You just have to have the satisfaction of the work—and your reputation in the industry."

"So I'm a masochist, satisfied with covert appreciation?"

"Your predilections are not my affair."

This divergence was almost touching but not very interesting. I broke in. "So you went on in the boat."

"Yes. And just on the other side of the block—or stream— from the firehouse—there's a guy literally swimming. Like he's in some giant, surreal pool. The rescuing angel at the helm yelled out to him, like he's coming to save a drowning man, but right away I sensed there was something else going on. This guy in the water was going on like he was swimming along the shore at the beach. He certainly wasn't drowning. We pulled alongside, our boatman, captain, rescue man whatever, said we could pull him in, but the guy just looked up at him— I think at the moment he was doing a breast stroke—and just said, 'I'm swimming.'

"The rescue man looked at this guy, looked at us, as if this was the most astonishing thing he could ever hear. This was Hurricane Harvey, fifty inches of rain, water was what everyone was afraid of, and here was this guy, well, embracing it. He was middle aged, forty-five, fifty, looked like, but in really good shape. The rain was still coming down, the water was still rising, and this guy just keeps swimming along. Our rescue man just stood, literally dumfounded. I was amused. And intrigued."

Blaise: "He was crazy. And that water wasn't clean. Wasn't there discharge from the sewers?"

"I think that was before that point. I think there was just the flood then, the rain that couldn't get absorbed by storm drains. But it was a flood, a deluge, a rain for the end of the world; and there's a guy just swimming along. We followed alongside him; it must have been for more than a half mile. What else could we do? I don't know how long he'd been swimming. Our rescue man was waiting for some sign of distress. Once in a while the swimmer looked up at us, back at us, smiled; though most of the time it seemed he was in his own world. And then he veers off, goes toward a house, a two-story house, with half of the first floor in water. The front door is open. And he *swims right into the house.* I swear. Now I'm a little dumbfounded myself. I tell the rescue man to go up to the door and we do. We're right at the doorway and I'm looking inside and I hear some, well, I guess swimming sounds and I call into the house. It was dim, you couldn't see much, and then suddenly the guy comes right around, swims back to us in this house, back to the doorway and says—as if he's answering the door in a normal world—says 'This is my house, you know.'

"And I just said, I was beginning to think of the whole practical aspect of this, 'So how long are you going to swim around in it?' He shot a hand up out of the water, gestured to stairs behind him. 'The second floor's OK.' I started to say something else, then he told us to go around the house, we could bring the boat right in, through the patio doors, they were open, he said. That's what we did. We floated right into his house. That was weird. You're boating right into a house—with high ceilings, so I guess it was easier to fit; and he's sitting halfway up the steps to the second floor, wiry guy, dripping wet—and right there I interviewed him a little. Weirdest interview setting I ever did an interview.

"His story fit the whole scene. He told me after the distress of his house being flooded, he just decided to swim around the neighborhood. He said that as if it were the most normal reaction you could have. He mentioned an old movie he'd seen, *The Swimmer*, from the 1960s, with Burt Lancaster (I Googled it), about a guy in some wealthy neighborhood who goes swimming from pool to pool, his neighbors' pools, and has all these strange interactions with the neighbors. He said that gave him the idea to do what he's been doing. 'I've been swimming off and on for a few hours, floating with the current—there is actually a current here—when I'm tired. But it's different than the movie. I'm not interacting with anyone.' Blaise asked him if he wanted to. He laughed. 'Probably not.'

"Our rescue man said, 'It's gonna be dark soon. You gonna be doing this at night?' The swimmer said he had some food upstairs, and that he'd probably swim over to the firehouse tomorrow. I remember he said, 'It's a certain sort of solitude I'm enjoying.'

Melissa shook her head, and echoed: "'A certain sort of solitude.' The rescue man said, 'You're taking your life in your hands.' The swimmer said, 'That's exactly what I'm doing.'" Melissa laughed. "That was basically the end of it, with the swimmer adding, 'I'm a careful swimmer.' And adding to that,

'Long as I don't get sucked down the basement.' He pointed to a door—it was open: the basement, which was flooded to the ceiling. That scared me. The entire house completely flooded below us, the first floor flooded enough for a small boat to float in it, and this guy telling us he had some food upstairs, he was going to hang out for the night and then swim over to the real world in the morning."

Blaise said, "I had a dream that night that our boat fell apart in the house, and there was a current in the water and it pulled us right into the basement, and I was in this black whirlpool and I was yelling out something, I wish I could remember what—then I woke up."

"To more adventures the next day."

"Yes," he said glumly.

Melissa: "So we left the swimmer there. He didn't seem in any distress. Though I did think he was a little crazy. You didn't know at that point if things were going to get even worse. The water did get more polluted: the septic systems overflowed, there were chemicals from industrial plants; there were those chemical explosions from plants without power that couldn't keep certain combustibles cool, something like that. I hope the swimmer did go to the firehouse the next day. We didn't see him again. But I was definitely left with this...this— feeling: something like Noah's flood comes upon us, and this guy think's it's a good day for a swim. Didn't know anything about his past; it's more than just seeing a movie that makes someone do something like that."

I said, "Maybe we need catastrophe to step outside of ourselves. Step outside of our lives."

Melissa shrugged. "Whatever. Or is that just meeting catastrophe with, well, narcissism? It's a Biblical flood, so I'll take a swim. We see the news, we see all these movies about catastrophe, but I wonder how much we can really comprehend catastrophe. We just think it's a big disruption, and then life will be getting on again. It did get on again, yeah...but maybe something is going to happen someday that it won't."

Melissa was quiet for a while, her face looking from us toward the lowered sun. A soft wind raised her hair. Blaise gave her an odd look, as if puzzled as to what she might say next, even if they had both worked through the ravages of that hurricane together. When she looked back at us Melissa gave a wry smile.

"The next morning, we were with a new rescue crew, evacuating a senior home. I don't know why they hadn't been taken care of sooner. The place was flooded. Not as bad as the swimmer's house, but bad enough. There were I don't know how many old people, stuck in the middle of at least a half a foot of water. You know how you hear about these places, that they stick people in front of the TV, the bingo table, and the old people who can hardly move, or who don't have the faculties to realize they should or even can move, stay there until the staff moves them. That's what it was like: statues of old people rising up in the water—well, more like those real life wax figures; but of course they were alive, and they were not understanding, it seemed, the flood at their ankles. That was like another end of the world vision for me: something that could drown you, kill you, just rising up at our feet, and we're just staying in place."

Melissa shook her head. "Is that what happens when you get old? Like you don't even seem *aware*?"

Rory said, "Maybe they were really far gone. Alzheimer's."

"Probably. Because I've seen a lot of old people who were a lot more aware than that."

I said, "Will any of us realize when we're old? I mean,

realize *that* we are old?"

"I will," said Rory.

"I will certainly deny it," said Blaise.

Melissa said, "As they were brought out into the light, and a lot more water than they'd been in inside, most of them seemed to come out of—what? Their daze? Whatever held them like statues in the water. Maybe they just needed to get *out* of that place, get away from bingo and TV. Well, they couldn't't've had TV just then, there was no power, but they must have been watching it, watching the weather reports, warnings, just before the storm; they had to know, even if vaguely, what was coming down. So the water had grown up around their ankles and now they were being ferried away in boats, and some of them, it seemed, looked at me as if they were starting to awake, their eyes registering something—"

"But was it reality?" said Blaise.

Melissa: "You getting metaphysical? That wasn't reality as usual, anyway. Maybe something like that registered. Surreality. Didn't I say that before? So they just sailed away, in several of these small boats, a bunch of passengers I guess not far from death in the first place, saved."

"But on the River Styx," I said.

"What?"

"Nothing. Never mind."

"Oh. That. Yeah. Anyway, I had to think, what would have happened if they'd been somewhere else, in the outback and they couldn't be reached for a while, for a long time? Would they just be sitting there, standing there, with the water rising?"

Blaise cut in: "We were in a boat with a few of them. This man, he was stooped over, and shaking a little—I couldn't tell if he was chilled by being in the water so long—it was a warm day—or if he just had Parkinson's or something. He had those dingy caps with the bill old people have, like some old golfing cap, and he just looked directly at me. I had just stopped filming for a minute. His eyes, even though his body was so…degraded—his eyes were clear. He was looking at me as if he wanted to ask me something. Then he just tilted back like he was going to fall, and someone caught him and helped him sit, and then he just looked out at the water, the flooded streets. Like his eyes were drowned in the water. Why that struck me so much I don't know."

"You wonder," I said, "how clear a memory they'll have of their rescue."

Melissa said, "Maybe they won't comprehend it as rescue: it'll be right there in their minds with bingo."

"No," said Blaise, "I think it'll be more…dreamlike than that."

Melissa: "A dream of a voyage?"

From some tangential reasoning that remark prompted me to say, "Jung said the water represents the unconscious—"

"Well, then Houston was a pretty unconscious place that week."

"Yes," said Blaise, "literally transcendent."

Melissa: "Blaise, that's snide—and not really accurate."

"Maybe you're weren't transcendent, but I might have been."

"You're not really the type, Blaise, don't kid yourself."

Blaise made a mock exasperated—and almost affectionate—noise; Melissa went on: "The weirder thing, though, was the prison."

Blaise: "I was astonished they did not evacuate prisoners."

Me: "Why didn't they?"

Melissa: "To where? A shelter? How are you going to police that? And you can't just take a thousand prisoners to another prison that's out of the flood zone. Most prisons are overcrowded as it is. Anyway, we're in this boat with some officials, and you turn this way and that in the flooded streets, and then there was a section where you didn't see flooded houses, it was like just water and out in the open; you really felt you were on some sort of sea, a newly created sea, and *that* felt scary, a feeling like the world you were familiar with, even though it was flooded, had fallen away from you, you were on some new sea world. I guess it was a flooded field. Then I saw this big structure in the distance. I saw it suddenly, though I should have been seeing it all along, with the water so flat and with nothing else but water around.

"We got closer and it's like we're passing across some giant moat to an ominous castle. Not a castle like the old castles, but those very ugly buildings that are just functional, not ornate like in the olden days, big brooding blocks of joined buildings—and inside…. We had to sort of dock at the gate, and get into smaller boats and just like we floated right into the swimmer's house we floated right into the prison. The ground floor was flooded. And you looked up at tiers of cellblocks, the men looking down, at the flood, at us, the visitors; and maybe, I thought, the water, the flood was a sort of safety for the people running the prison: the prisoners were not going to try to escape, to come down into the flood. I thought the prisoners might have felt even more trapped. They could have thought the water was going to keep rising, a surreal (OK, that word again), surreal deluge, right up to the top of the tiers and their jailers were going to let them drown. Some guy screamed down at us, 'I can't swim!' Maybe he was being sarcastic, or just sincerely hysterical, I couldn't tell."

Blaise said, "It made me think of some kind of Noah's Ark, with prisoners instead of animals. In fact, a lot of them made sort of animal noises as I filmed them. I once had to do an ag film in a slaughterhouse: branded and tagged animals waiting for—you know. In a place that had no mercy. Noah's Ark at least had a happy ending."

I was quiet a moment, absorbing that terrible analogy, then Melissa suddenly laughed. "Meanwhile our tour guide—and that's what he was—this little bald guy, whose eyelids fluttered when you tried to make eye contact with him, who looked too vulnerable to be working in a prison, was assuring us, 'These men are being taken care of, we've got supplies—' Etc."

Blaise said, "I asked if the toilets were working. They weren't expecting that question."

Melissa: "Yeah, what did make you think of that?"

Blaise shrugged. "The guy told me, 'Of course. So far, at least. Anyway, gravity always helps.' I asked him what did he exactly mean? He said, 'Well, it all has to come down hill, sort of.' That just gave me an image of the flood at the bottom of the prison being filled with feces—and I thought I just wanted to get back out into the air."

Melissa: "I didn't see any sea of excrement around, but then there was this plastic bottle floating, bumped up against the boat, and it had a paper rolled up in it, I swear: yeah, message in a bottle; and our guide was really surprised and frowning as I picked it up. I was a soda bottle with a screw top. I unscrewed it, and edge of the paper was right up near the top of the bottle. I pulled the paper out. It just said, 'God is drowning the world again.'"

Blaise: "See? Noah's Ark."

Melissa: "Our guide's eyelids fluttered and he took the bottle and the paper from me. I just said, for some reason, 'It's not signed.'" She shook her head, squinted further into the by now very much lowered sun, just about to touch the horizon. I imagined a floating prison, out here, in the midst of the Pacific. I thought the nearing future might find floating prisons on these high seas, not at all the ark of Noah, but outcast internment cities of the new millennium.

Melissa said, "We were there about an hour. We walked around the tiers. Some of the men looked back at us with no expression, others gave us very nasty—deadly—looks; some cursed, one yelled out, 'Is there going to be more rain?' I told him the rain was ending. He said to me, 'What if you're lying?' That took me aback. 'Why should I be?' I said. 'Because you're free,' he said. That took me even more aback. So those who are free...lie? I just said, 'You can look out the window.' That might have been cruel: you know, barred windows—"

She paused, went on: "We interviewed a few of the men. I'm not sure if they were handpicked for us to interview—"

Blaise: "It did seem at random."

Melissa paraphrased the inmate. "What if that was a lie?" Blaise shrugged. Melissa said, "Three guys. They were basically calm. It seemed their biggest complaint was losing TV—"

Rory interjected. "If you took TV away from our culture there'd be a revolt. Or a collapse."

Melissa seemed indifferent to the prospect of the arena of her livelihood been stricken by some new turn of history. She said, "I almost thought, talking to these men, they seemed too calm. Here they were, locked up, and the water had to seem a threat. Even though most of them could not have thought it was going to rise up that far and drown them. I know I kept looking down at that flooded first floor of the prison. Anyway, I guess it was like every neighborhood: there was a...*temporary* lack of services. None of the men I interviewed said anything really memorable. I had the feeling they'd watched so many people interviewed on TV, especially those one or two sentences people on the street are allowed when they're interviewed for the news, that they had absorbed those sound bites of, well, not really conversation, I mean, not really anything…original to say."

I said: "You wanted oratory?"

Melissa virtually scowled at me. "You know what I mean."

She was quiet for a few moments. "The *piece de resistance*, I guess, in light of what we were doing here, now, was the water bottles. Hurston would appreciate this. There was no running water in the prison; they had trucked in—or sailed in—I don't know how many water bottles for the prison. Were there a thousand people in there? Those sixteen-ounce water bottles, the thin plastic crunchy kind. Our guide said there was the worry (he said 'Off the record—') the prisoners could 'weaponize' the plastic somehow. Captivity forces ingenuity, I guess. We saw some, well, more than some of those five gallon big containers for water coolers—for the staff, I guess, but by far more of the small water bottles—days' worth, piled in every corner. Well, maybe not literally: with the prison flooded, you didn't really have corners, at least at ground level. You can't say that where water meets a wall is really a corner. The bottles had been collected in these giant black plastic garbage bags. They were tied somehow, and floating on top of the water. I didn't like the way the garbage bags rose and fell slightly, like body bags on a tide, a current.

"We met the warden. He was in wading boots and a sweaty shirt. He more interviewed me than I did him. 'Are they saying this is going to drain away soon?' He asked. I told him I had no idea. He looked at me as if I was, well, if not lying, then hiding information I had to know. I tried to joke, 'I'm not the weatherman.' He didn't seem to like that.

"His office was high above the flood—or maybe it was a temporary office, I don't know. There was a window where you could see the flooded plain we'd come across. There was a sunny, cloudy light on the water—as if the water was suffused with a light you could not receive inside the prison. That…desolation looked like a paradise compared to this place we'd entered.

"He told me that before the storm he'd been prepared to be 'trapped in here' a little while, 'But now it could be a week, if you look at this water.' I didn't know if he was looking to me for sympathy. All I could say, and I felt stupid saying it, was 'How have the prisoners been?' He seemed disturbed at that question, like it was something I shouldn't've brought up. 'Good—so far. Maybe the…unusualness' (he made that word sound too formal) 'of the situation…has kept them in check. But I can't see…if it's going to be *days*…. I've requested more help, more correctional officers. But I don't see that coming—for a while.'"

"We talked a while. It turned out this warden—God, I forgot his name—was, I guess you could say, progressive. He had brought in all these special programs for the prisons: from literacy to learning to be mechanics to drama. 'A lot of them may be pretty bad people, but almost all of them have had…well, constricted lives,' he said. "You know how many prisoners come back into the system; I'd like to make it a little less.'

"So he was a good guy. Though he was mocked by some of his peers. He told me another warden had said to him, 'What's next, ballet?' I don't know if it was the same warden, but he'd also been told, since the storm, 'Well I guess it rained on your parade.' He laughed at that: the kind of laugh you laugh when you're angry. 'It's raining on everybody's parade! Isn't that crazy?'

"Well, even after all he had done, after we left I heard that there had been an unsuccessful, well, sort of revolt by the prisoners; I guess a storm like that…the prisoners had to face they were still locked up, with the water maybe rising. Anyway, the water policed them more than the guards. There was actually one death: a prisoner drowned. (Was it the one who said he couldn't swim?) It was under investigation. There were accounts that he had *been* drowned. That was never proven. I'm pretty sure the issue was dropped. Never heard anything more about it."

She abruptly added: "Oh, yeah, as we were leaving, some prisoner shouts out, 'Where you gonna swim to now?' I turned around, couldn't tell who'd shouted that, just yelled back to all those faces in tiers above the flood: 'No swimming, taking a boat!' There was this…unsettling laughter—and hooting."

* * *

 After being quiet a while, Melissa added, "We were there, in Texas, long enough to see the floods recede—a little—"

Blaise: "I had the feeling when we left we'd survived, everyone had survived…something like a warning."

Melissa: "Blaise, I never realized you were so…."

"What?"

She shrugged. "I don't know." She sighed, tilted her head back, surrendered her face to that horizontal, burnished, sun setting light.

Blaise said, "Let's say I can be aware of…heralds."

Melissa straightened her head, opened her eyes. After a moment she said, "Heralds. After Harvey there was Irma, Jose, Maria, one after the other. The oceans are definitely getting warmer, creating more and bigger storms. I turned down the opportunity to cover those. Harvey had been enough for me."

Blaise said, playfully now, "One does not need a plethora of heralds."

13.

Had the Buddhas floating in the middle of the Pacific been heralds?

We weren't at the center yet, and there was a bit more madness to go through. I fell asleep early that night, got up early—the sun only a little above the horizon, but already blazing—and went up on deck. I saw something more than a little astonishing. Or maybe it shouldn't've been. Rita stretched out on a towel *naked*—before the Buddhas.

One Buddha was immediately before her. In diverging lines from that Buddha, others fanned out, like ordered flanks of a ritual retinue. Rita's eyes were closed, her face peaceful. There was a slight smile to her lips—which seemed to increase as she certainly heard my step.

"Hello," she said, her eyes still closed, and without knowing whom it was. Though *did* she know my step?

"What the hell are you doing?"

"Sunbathing. Relaxing." Eyes still closed.

"Naked in public?"

"Public? We're thousand miles from nowhere." Eyes still closed.

"Come on. You don't care when the men come up?"

She opened her eyes and looked at me. "I think they can handle it."

"Oh, I'm sure they can handle being aroused."

There was a little laugh. "You think I'm an exhibitionist?"

"I wouldn't've thought it—but maybe that's what your

sarcasm is."

That was the end of that exchange. Emile and Jorges came on deck. Emile made some choking sound in his throat and Jorges made a happy screech in Spanish. Rita closed her eyes and went back into her Buddha-ness, her sun soaking defiance. (What the hell was it, but defiance?) The two men stood there, eyes, as they say, wide. As men they were certainly struck by Rita's body, as crewmembers, normal human beings, they didn't know what to do, how to act. When Hurston came up on deck and exclaimed "My God!" and Rita responded with a short laugh, I went back below.

It was Blaise who told me the rest. He had been summoned on deck by Melissa ("She was sort of crazy, but almost happy—") who'd come up to find Rita and Hurston arguing and of course had gotten Blaise to save it for posterity. "Though I couldn't see even Melissa using it," Blaise said. And added that Rita was not so much arguing as letting him rant, "calling her exhibitionist," with Rita saying only a little back, such as "Let your senses be a little freer."

"That made him madder," said Blaise. "He looked stunned. He stepped back—then he leaned back to her, right into her, put his face in hers, and screamed—and I mean screamed—'What do you mean *freer*?'"

Blaise said Rita and Hurston looked at each other for a long time. Rory had come out on deck. As Blaise recounted, "He laughed. 'I guess this is the nude beach section,' he said. To me Rita was baiting Hurston—cruelly—about his apparent (I guess not unexpected) desire for her. And I thought maybe she wanted him, was goading him—and thought she had to be blatant to do it."

Me: "To get him from the fiancée?"

"Yeah. Just to do it, not really want him."

Rita didn't answer the question about "freeness." Hurston hurled another furious question: "Why don't you just tie yourself to your ship like your mannequin?"

Rita's answer: "All that exposure wouldn't be good for my skin."

"I'm sure she made them all tent poles," laughed Blaise. He told me Hurston had spun around, ordered everyone below deck. Emile and Jorges had retreated, smirking. "Rory said he was being Captain Bligh. I knew the name but I couldn't—" I explained the reference to Blaise. He said, "I think Captain Bligh would have enjoyed her himself. He—our captain— cursed at me and my camera; and I was feeling that Melissa was forcing me into a peep show. And Hurston cursed at Melissa, telling her she was on board only with his permission; he didn't want this sort of thing on any documentary. Melissa was cool, I have to say. She just said to him, 'I just see one of your research workers sunbathing, that's all' But we all packed it in when Hurston screamed at us. Even Melissa didn't want to deal with that. We left him and her on deck. "Maybe he did want to…" Blaise stopped, with a grin.

"The way of all flesh?"

"Well, we walk around with it, that's what it is."

*   *   *

I wrote something about Hurston that day:

Our captain grew up in various places along the coast of California, with parents who were both "pioneers" (as he put it) in the computer industry ("before it really took off"). His was both a semi-nomadic life and a sheltered one, for the father had inherited a bit of money from some not so distant New England relation. While growing up, Hurston had been subject to the overt forces of a new technology and the more unconscious influences of a moneyed New England past, a character of which there are threads in him today, the yachting playboy turned eco-savior. Of course, that growing up on the California coast, becoming immersed in the surfing life, made him naturally love the visceral pull of the ocean, this vast, vast Pacific whose shores on this side rolled to Los Angeles and San Francisco and San Diego and on the other curve of the world touched the cliché-labeled inscrutable East—and which, in this century, had become another thing entirely.

So the young man had surfed and sailed, then yachted, using his share of now what was more than one inheritance to design and sell a better surf board and faster sail boats. The sea was not only in his daily life, its sun and waters touched his skin, but it was in his money—and so perhaps his present mission was as much self defense as it was the proverbial "giving back" to the world that had been good to him (at least good *for* him).

He did speak about the water, the ocean with love, and you had to love him for that—well, at least like him, respect him. He had taken a passion and was seeing its problems—at least most of its problems—clearly. The person who had been "a surfer kid" had gone beyond the day's pleasure of the big wave, had gone beyond the satisfying ventures into the business of gathering pleasure from the waters, and had understood something dark about the slow and steady pollution of the seas girdling the Earth.

Now in his midforties, Hurston had that look that used to be called ruggedly handsome (is that still a label?), but after being around him I thought any woman at first drawn to Hurston would ultimately suffer a distant second to the focus of his obsessions.

In conversation with him once, I'd been surprised he not only minutely detailed humankind's depredations in the Pacific, but spoke knowingly about environmental violations all over the Earth—land, sea, and sky. The last with a hint of conspiracy: "They are dumping things in the air we don't know about," he said. "Chemtrails. You'll get a million facts about them on the internet—" Then a laugh. "Though not *the* fact…."

Before I could ask him about that emphasis he said, "People used to tell me 'they' are putting things in the food, the air—mind control, make us crazy." He shook his head. "We've always been mad. Look at our religions: *our* explanations. But now it seems—just think of this: when I was younger—maybe not you—you wouldn't hear about people walking into their job or a school and shooting as many people as they could. Then themselves."

I said, "Like the insanity of the race focused ten times in one person."

He looked at me with happy surprise. "Exactly! A violence of one magnified to—to a whole society. Like the Nazis."

"The Nazis were a long time ago."

"The Nazis were a structure. The devil likes structure—" I was so surprised at Hurston going on like this. "What happens now…it's one person becoming the Nazi state."

"So—its chemtrails doing this?"

"Probably all the mix. Pollution, hormones in the food, violence in the instantaneous media, children being given drugs because it appears they can't sit still—for the structure. Hell, I was a kid who didn't want to sit still. I wanted to *move*."

Just then some shards of plastic floated by *The Argus*, Hurston smiled at me, ruefully. "Garbage is quiet—undemanding. The leftover of what was functional. Or was *that* functional?" He gestured to the bobbing plastic.

I squinted at these remnants of something. "I can't tell what it was."

"Neither can I. Was it needed though? That's the question."

"Needs are subjective."

"The more you have, yes. A hungry belly isn't subjective. It's we convince ourselves what we have to do to feed the belly—I mean, feed other than the belly."

The debris was floating past *The Argus*. As the portion of it, wet with the ocean, reflected the light; it seemed to me the fragment of an enigma. Of our evil, our wants, and perhaps of a self deluded act: making an object that would be good—for someone. But—useful? Isn't that the biggest question we face? What's useful? Faith or love—or anything? Hurston was making himself useful, that he did believe. I have to say I believed he was, too.

*   *   *

The rest of the day was an uneasy one on *The Argus*. When I came back on deck I noted only three Buddhas in sight. I found out that Rory had taken two of them below—and Hurston had thrown the rest of them overboard. I visualized him doing this with a quiet fury; I wondered if he had ascertained their functionality or lack thereof.

It seemed we were all keeping to ourselves, like members of a family embarrassed at a quarrel that had erupted in our midst and had pushed us into stupid responses. Not that the scene between Hurston and Rita had actually been what you could call a quarrel.

When I thought on it I came up with this: Beginning with Langhorn, a refuge after a storm, our coming upon Smith's plastic islands, the mannequin, the Buddhas—it was all too awash with strangeness. I think that was what Hurston had been voicing—protesting—consciously or unconsciously; a resentment at how his very logical quest to research the Great Pacific Garbage Patch and come up with ways in which our species could keep from fouling the ocean had been confronted by one bizarre mockery after another. Or, going deeper, it could be that Hurston and the rest of us might now be thinking there was something bizarre about *The Argus'* mission in the first place, something awry just below the surface of the politically correct purpose that had to inevitably lead to further exaggeration of itself.

It's not good to think too much like this. It paralyzes intent and actions. For some time that afternoon I stood by the ship's railing and watched high tech trash flow by, not in a clump, as with the Buddhas, but here and there, scattered, separated, but constant. High and low tech. Something that looked like part of a dashboard from a car, and, as if in mimicry, a little toy truck, of a once bright red, bleached with the elements, with faded yellow wheels; part of a beach umbrella, a black plastic ladle.... I was trying to consider if the size of the trash was diminishing, as we should be getting closer to the center of the patch, with plastic—with whatever material—more degraded with time; the plastic so broken down that we'd eventually see few objects as discernible as that toy truck—but it seemed we still had some way to go for that.

Though I did note, that afternoon, my first dead fish. I'm far from expert at identifying one fish from another, so I couldn't say what type of fish it was: a half foot in length, maybe, floating dead with its white belly shining in the sun. Speaking of heralds, that had to be one, I thought, this fish somewhere on the food chain that could very likely have been ingesting minute plastic debris or who had eaten other fish who had eaten plastic. Or maybe it had simply died of natural causes. How could I know? But I was geared for *something* to happen that was...expected.

14.

I paid Rory a visit, his small cabin crammed with various scraps of plastic taken from the waters, including the two Buddhas. "Nothing extraordinary about these," Rory said to me, "other than the fact they are Buddhas floating in the middle of the ocean."

The Buddhas were dry now, and looked too much the mundane copy of some holy art. Actually, I've never cared much for Eastern art in the first place, with its unattractive renditions of the body. Western art, in which the Greeks and Romans had celebrated the body, had had its own stretch of sensuality and fleshly vigor corrupted by the emaciated holy art of the Middle Ages, whose Christs and prophets and martyrs had been ugly and muscleless, testament to the alleged uselessness and powerlessness of the flesh before the eternal divinity of the spirit. The Renaissance had returned the divine to the flesh. Look at Michelangelo's David, the bodybuilder-like physique of the horned Moses. Then again, for the past century or so, most contemporary artists had steered away from the exactness and power of the flesh, rendering a brooding abstract—or commercial—inner world so that the icons of flesh of this prolonged era were, say, (to use him again) Warhol's Monroe, who relayed to us only a cartoon seductiveness. Ironically, perhaps only pornography, given its expanse into the mainstream by *Playboy* in the 1950s and the internet in the 1990s, brought the power of the body back into consistent view. But, being pornography, it sought the venal and not the profound; it could not be regarded as art. If today a sculptor lets loose a David, the poor artist is mocked as lacking—in vision, purpose, even skill.

I have to also consider the vast scope of sub-Saharan African art, once little regarded by the West—which had the perspective that African art was not art for art's sake, but created for more functional than aesthetic purposes. But logic says that whatever a cultural milieu inflicts upon artists, there will always be those who see their creations as things in themselves as well as being integrated into the life of their place and time. The Sistine Chapel's heavenscape had its prime purpose as functional: to awe the viewer with the divine creation the Church's authority oversaw. Anyway, African art ranged from what might be called primitive, to the most modern, post-modern abstract expressionism, and, in that continuum, very realistic busts and paintings. While African masks are a subject in themselves.

If I wanted to be rigorous in my honesty, I'd say that the closest thing to art among Smith's islands, the Buddhas, and the mannequins was Rita's naked body on the deck, the mundane Buddhas more the poor acolyte to this woman's beauty than the other way around. Rita did take care of her flesh—unlike myself. She had told me she did yoga every morning and throughout the year alternated between aerobics, weight training and swimming, though I wonder if she would admit that all her efforts didn't so much create her incredible form as maintain and embellish it—as well as display it. I'd been given an average body, and so my body was my vehicle, not my essence. Of course, being a citizen of the modern age, especially a woman of the 21st century, I was given the option of cosmetic transformation, implant this, suck away that, a casual remodeling of bone, the inner architecture that insists on itself so that it shows even through the flesh, but—not yet. Perhaps when age takes away the advantage of youth; perhaps when I have the money.

*   *   *

Rory's cabin was messy with shards of plastic, tools, a microscope, computer, a disarray of books. Like Hurston he expressed his eagerness to get to the center of the Patch, though for not exactly the same reasons. He suddenly began to explain to me this wild theory of his, though I don't think he would have called it a theory out loud, just something that was intriguing speculation.

"Plastic may be artificial, our construct, but…I wonder: if broken down so thoroughly, by water, sunlight, digested by fish—if all this could exert some sort of change in the structure of plastic. Now if you go with evolution, science's official dogma, *the animate grew out of the inanimate*—somehow. Silica, clay—" He had a little laugh, as if to himself. "Like in the Bible: from clay, dust: a man—life. Somehow, organic compounds: *then* organic. I wondered if plastic could be wrought by all this into—"

"Life?" I was curious at how far out he was reaching.

"Oh, I wouldn't necessarily say *that*…. Just—a different plastic. Or you could say…if DNA, RNA came out of the inanimate, maybe something at least *replicating*. Doesn't have to be alive, just—"

"Reproducing."

"You could use that word."

"Like the way they say computers—machines—will reproduce?"

"I've thought," Rory said, "and I don't go around telling this to everyone—people expect a scientist to be staid—maybe our function, the human race, I mean, is as a catalyst. We make things. We started with pots and arrowheads—probably spears before that; or clubs. Clubbed each other with rocks before clubs. Then we made machines that could mass produce other machines, parts, whatever. A sort of natural evolution. Now here, even when we cast off what we don't want, in the primal soup it becomes—" He stopped himself, perhaps tried to be a bit staid: "If it's possible….."

"Then you'd prefer the Garbage Patch to continue to exist—plastic primal soup."

"Maybe on a small scale—controlled. For study."

I laughed, he laughed, too. But his laugh said: *Think about.* I said to him, "Tell me—why plastics?"

"What?"

"Why'd you go into your field? There's that old movie—ever see *The Graduate*? Some know-it-all businessman tells a kid out of college—how does it go: 'One word for you—plastics.'"

"Never saw the movie; I heard the line. I didn't go into plastics for some visionary outcome."

"Sounds like you have one now."

"I don't know." He seemed uncomfortable with the word "visionary."

"You think Hurston's a visionary?"

"A playboy who's had a revelation. Not that he isn't sincere. And not that there isn't a real problem with plastics."

"So it is visionary for you now."

"A little. You begin to see past…the basic stuff…."

Then, perhaps to divert from any personal passion he had revealed, told me something of the history of plastics.

"Plastics," he began, actually shaking his head, as if it was such a large topic he doubted he could convey all of it to me—and that I could take it all in. "When you think about it, plastic has displaced too many materials that people have been using for centuries: wood, glass, bone, metal, horn, ceramics, leather. It's in cars, spaceships, paper clips. Cars today are about 20 percent plastic. There are polymer implants in our bodies.

Incidentally, if you are thinking of plastic surgery, that's not named for literal plastics, but for what the word means: something that you can shape and reshape."

He went on: "You could call what Mesoamericans were doing in 1600 B.C., using natural rubber for figurines and balls in their games, as a use of plastic. In the Middle Ages they combined casein, that milk protein, with lye, and they produced something that was window-like, used it in lanterns.

"It was an inevitable segue from the natural, the organic to the synthetic. There was Goodyear's vulcanization of rubber, which led to tires for bicycle, then tires for cars; and transatlantic cables. And then the first real manmade plastic, Parkesine: nitrocellulose—from Alexander Parkes in the UK, in 1862. He mixed cellulose from plants and nitric acid. You could make combs, buttons, knife handles for it. You molded it in alcohol and hardened it into an elastic—and transparent—material when heated. You could color it. Usually they made it to look like ivory.

"Parkes tried to market his discovery, but was a better scientist than businessman—who isn't? Two Americans, the Hyatt brothers, took what Parkes had done, added camphor, which made the Parkesine more easily shaped, and there you go: celluloid. So by 1870 you had the basis for the 20th century film industry.

"At the end of the 1800s there was galalith; you probably never heard of that. Another horn-like plastic from casein. Originally chemists were trying to make a blackboard substitute, but they came up with casein mixed with formaldehyde.

"Formaldehyde was essential in the first real synthetic plastic: Bakelite. A Belgian chemist, Leo Baekeland, use phenol and formaldehyde. So now we had a plastic that had no plant or animal components, but was derived from petrochemicals.

"Things went faster after that, like everything in the 20th century. Especially with WWII. Those polymers like polystyrene, polyvinyl chloride (they made that back in 1872, but it wasn't mass produced until the 1920s). You had plastic resins, polyethylene, polypropylene, polystyrene—for insulation, cups, packaging—"

I asked, "Explain all the 'poly' words."

"Oh. A polymer. Long chains of repetitive molecules with a high molecular mass, mostly made out of carbon."

"Isn't carbon the basis for all life?"

"That's what they say."

I said, "I heard somebody at a conference describe polymers like a bicycle chain: you click one molecule onto the other, as long as you want. Silicone falls into this category, as well, as, yeah, DNA."

"Exactly," said Rory. He outlined how World War II really drove the development and use of plastic. "They were in radar insulation and military vehicles. Oil companies were turning oil into plastic; and then, with war's end, they had the facilities to make so much plastic, they went from the military to the consumer market. Ubiquitous Tupperware came in 1948.

"So now milk bottles, cups, dishes were being made of different types of plastic. You just tweak the polymers this way and that. The problem became, the problem is, what we now have: plastic is forever. There are no organisms that break down, that digest these synthetic materials.

"You could say our water bottle curse began in the WWII era with polyethylene terephthalate (PET) being used as a replacement for glass bottles. Finally, there is a movement to make biodegradable plastics—sort of going back the way we came. Polylactic acid from corn starch: plastic bags, clothing, even, that can degrade. Pepsi and Coke were in competition to produce the first fully bioplastic PET bottle. Pepsi took it. Yeast from sugar cane goes through stages: into ethylene, polythene, then PET. What we hope is that the big oil companies will see the profit in going this route."

He sighed, scratched his chin and looked reflective. "When I said there is certainly a problem with plastics.... All that science I just related is giving us horrendous pollution. All over the world we're finding micro particles of plastic in water. I just saw a study from a dozen countries that found plastic particles in 83 percent of tap water. America was the worst: 94 percent of tap water samples had plastic particles. Microplastic absorbs toxic chemicals before we ingest the particles; and those chemicals are released when we consume them.

"It's at the very bottom of the marine food chain. This whole ocean needs plankton; let me show you this—" He produced a photo of plankton filled with polystyrene particles bulging against transparent flesh. "The particles are less than 50 nanometers long. They've filled the entire insides of the plankton, like a virus about to burst through a cell.

"It's not just in the ocean but lakes. Lake Victoria in Africa has plastic particles in 20 percent of the fish. That lake provides drinking water for 430 million people. There's a recent study that found that practically all the sea turtles in the world have plastic particles in their stomachs.

"And years ago, I read a study from Indonesia that found— it was a small sampling, but pretty ominous—plastics in umbilical cords. Indonesia is one of the major plastic polluters; China is the worst. In the poorer parts of these countries, millions of people cook their food over burning plastic. In America we may not be cooking our food over plastic garbage, but the plastic pollution we produce makes us one of the world's leaders.

"We're waking up to this too slowly. As of yet there is no international 'safe threshold' for plastic in water, in food. It seems impossible to escape our own creation. Plastic fibers escape from acrylic blankets. Plastic dust from carpets, cables, vinyl siding and flooring. It's pretty certain these particles absorb toxic chemicals from the air just as plastic particles do in water.

"Water treatment systems cannot filter out plastic nanofibers; they're too small. Like with the plankton, these fibers travel throughout the entire body. They go right through the walls of the intestine, into organs, the lymphatic system. It gets into everything from bottled water—of course you know that—to bottled beer.

"It's obvious we have to recycle: to produce plastic from the plastic that's already there. Sort of zero population growth for plastic. But even if the amount of plastic in the world does not increase starting today, there is still too much of it here: in the water and the air."

I said, "So would you want zero growth for plastic, or to discover self replicating plastic?"

He gave a big laugh at that. "Don't prod the mad scientist weakness in me. That could be an ugly wound."

15.

We sailed on. As the sun seemed to stamp a constant countenance of heat and light upon the sea, we saw less and less of the larger debris and more dead marine life. My dead fish had been a harbinger. Fish floating belly up. There was one large fish with a jellyfish in its mouth and a plastic bag, desiccated into a gossamer shroud, entwined around the jellyfish—a compression of the image of human inflicted death upon the animal and primeval world. Rita, the lovely nude of the ship's art, was much less sardonic now and related facts about the depredation plastic inflicted on marine life. Melissa had Blaise bend close over these dead fish, which had been hauled up on deck, their eyes set in unseeing, and zoom in with his camera, while Rita intoned in the background, as the newswoman in turn intoned her dire politically correct notes: "How extensive is the pollution of our waters, our oceans? And can it be reversed?" Her face, artfully done, her hair blown back perfectly by the wind, just enough to suggest she braved a rugged setting in which Nature could not unhinge her. Well, she was attractive and chastising. I mean, attractive in the general sense, to her invisible, eventual viewers. Any previous thoughts I'd had about Melissa making the best of the situation she was in, the role she had to play as a commercial newswoman, were pushed to the rear of my opinions. She had chosen her path. I too had chosen to report news, the news of science, the science which in this case Melissa reported so stereotypically— Then I caught myself in my arrogance, swirled in all too obvious profundities; and did inner apologies by tainting my new friendliness toward Blaise with the fact that he had chosen *his* path…. I guess none of us were "pure" here.

As we moved toward the center of the Patch, and there were further indications of the marine dead, Hurston grew more taciturn and basically uncommunicative. Again, Smith's islands had been a distraction from the knight's quest; then the mannequin, the Buddhas—and Rita's nude defiance; our captain sulked in a pique I could both understand and criticize. Did he ever really think his "good works" would go untainted, uncorrupted by the hubris usually inherent in "good works"? –

And the irregular events such works seem to attract? The two Buddhas were still on deck, and the ravaged mannequin was still lashed to the bow; the Buddhas tumbled here and there in their forever lotus postures, the former our seeming guide, a blind oracle, poised and moving just above the debris that was in substance so like itself. I suppose I translated some of this image of mine into Hurston's psyche; I often caught him staring at the mannequin sullenly—or thoughtfully. Did he imagine the inanimate copy of a human being could "see," in a way, the inanimate scope of the pollution that directly affected the animate world? Yes, these were my wild thoughts, which I did not attempt to save from irrationality.

*   *   *

We came nearer to the center of the Patch. The weather grew hotter. It was a day of torpor. The air was thick and heavy, the sun blinding. Melissa complained that the air conditioner below deck wasn't adequate—though she put it more bluntly, with a few expletives. Hurston had always cautioned us there were limits to the power the solar panels could give us—even with so much sun and sky above. Anyway, we were all suffering from the heat, if each of us did not voice it so bluntly. There might have been an unfortunate, unconscious connection with this physical discomfort and our approach to the center of the Patch, but those feelings went wholly unspoken.

Hurston sweated like the rest of us.

In the afternoon, when the heat was at its worst, I caught this half smile (almost a smirk) from our captain as he looked westward, at our journey toward the center of the debris, and then an odd look—which afterwards I concluded was one of a sort of satisfaction. It made me ask him what he was thinking.

"I was remembering when I was really cold. I'll take this

heat over that."

"And when were you really cold?"

So he told this story—directly to me, but Emile and Jorges were in earshot, and soon they stopped their work to listen. And Rory and Rita happened to come on deck shortly after Hurston began. Melissa and Blaise didn't have the benefit (if that's the word) of hearing it in Hurston's own words; I was the one who filled them in later.

"It was about three years ago," said Hurston. "I took part for a while in this experiment: of living on a glacier that circled the currents of the Artic. A giant iceberg. It was just before I got involved in *this*—" He gestured to the warm, hardly moving sea, marked with its stilled pastiche flotsam. When I recalled that remark later, I understood that the adventure on the floating glacier was a deep indication that Hurston had wanted to turn his life to something deeper.

"The glacier was like a slice of land—with flat surfaces, little hills, even a harbor; ice instead of dirt and grass. It was large—eight miles wide, ten long. There was already a scientific base operating on it before I got there. My qualifications—well, they weren't scientific. I made a donation to the work—which was twofold (the work, not the donation): tracing the glacier through the currents, and to see how well people could live—and do research—in that environment. Which I thought had already been proven; there have been scientists living and working in Antarctica for decades. But I guess floating around the Artic was different.

"At times we sighted Greenland, Iceland, eastern Canada. One of the scientists said, 'It's like we're on some frozen ship in a story from Poe. There was something he'd written, his longest story, about some artic horror.' Hurston smiled and nodded. "It was like that. I came with their regular supply shipment and for the next two months there was no contact with the rest of the world. I mean no physical contact. There was radio, the internet when we could get it.

"I helped the scientists with their work, lugging equipment around in the cold. I climbed hills of ice. The austere beauty of those vistas—" He gave a slight shudder; memory had taken him from the heat of today's sun into that frozen world. "Anyway: one afternoon I had a slight accident: slipped, went sliding down into a little ravine. I was stupid. I'd gone out alone; that violated the rule of always going out in at least pairs. I guess I'm the stupid individualist.

"It wasn't like I almost died. I was there—an hour?—hour and a half?—before they got me out. Of course, I was in the most advanced artic gear, but I got cold, very cold. Because I couldn't even stand up. My body was half jammed into the ice; could barely move. I thought about the old explorers—without this gear, no radio. I looked up at the sky—it was just as blue as this sky, but it was as cold as this is hot." He smiled at us. "I'd rather sweat than shiver.

"When I got back inside I felt half numb for hours. After that, when I was outside—and I went outside cautiously the next day, as if something might bite me out there—I really felt the danger, the threat. Take just some of that clothing away, the supplies, and you wouldn't live."

He looked at each of us, as if expecting an argument—or some sort of grim agreement. "Some of the researchers thought you *could* survive—without the modern. There were seals and polar bears that visited the glacier from time to time. Someone killed a seal—for food. Some of us argued about that being illegal. I saw the skinned seal; I saw them cooking it. Barbaric. Actually, it affected me like the cold. When I came back I became a vegetarian; and stayed in warmer seas. We are closer to—something; something not modern—than we think. That guy who killed the seal—was it the one who'd mentioned Poe?; I'm not sure—told me that in the last century, beginning of the 1900s, some polar expedition had lived off artic game while they had stayed on a floating glacier like this for months. Hardly used their supplies. Maybe it's a little frightening how well we survive. At least survive; I don't know if it's always survive well."

When I gave my own recounted version to Melissa and Blaise the next day the newswoman smirked, "Our always daring captain," and Blaise said, "God, cold like that would be madness." I brought that back to Hurston who said, "There is a madness about the extremes of Nature. Though that just seems that way to us—to life. Whether it's polar bears in the Artic or hominids from Africa, we've got our climate niche— a narrow one. If we go out of it: death. Unless you've got the proper gear. I conclude—it's nothing profound—Nature regards life indifferently—or doesn't regard it. Life's an accident among the elements—and has to beware of them."

*   *   *

Another vignette of horror, but more of the B movie type than Poe, was very shortly encountered.

We ran into a veritable island of jellyfish, easily a few hundred yards in any direction, their gathered bodies made ominous by sheer number.

"God," said Blaise, "*that* is scary."

"Expected," said Rita.

We'd seen several clusters of jellyfish on our voyage, and Rita had dropped a few facts about the apparent increase of their population as a direct result of pollution and overfishing, but until entering this vast stretch of the creatures—*The Argus* was already touching the vast stretch of that "island"—these were just eco-disaster facts like all the others. Since the midpoint of the 20th century, since the bomb, I guess, we've all lived with the impending scenario of worldwide disaster: WWIII, ecological collapse, the population explosion, even the totalitarian step of the New World Order; and we're still here. Here, if in a bit of a mess, yes, but here.

But now, as we slowly made our way through this huge mass of semi-transparent creatures, their domed bodies both lost to definition in the water yet glinting sporadically in the sun, with their trailing threads of poisonous tentacles, the weight of the possibilities these ancient and odd sea animals presented made me in take in what Rita said; she was repeating what she had already told us and was adding a good deal. Hurston came up beside us—all of us were together, listening to Rita, while Blaise filmed the spectacle.

"With so much of the fish that fed on them overfished, with warming oceans, some scientists predict jellyfish will become the dominant marine life. They've actually shut down nuclear power plants by clogging cooling equipment that opens out into water, stung and killed thousands of fish in fisheries. We make the waters more acidic—jellyfish love it. The more we heat and acidify, the more jellyfish reproduce. Some species can produce 45,000 eggs a day. There are 1,500 species, in all sizes. Thumbnail to huge. Some have tentacles that are a hundred feet long."

The tentacles of the jellyfish that were lapping at the hull of *The Argus* were hardly that length, but they were, I'd say, a good five to six feet. Long enough to wrap around a swimmer.

We were now well into the island of jellyfish. The progress of *The Argus* had definitely slowed. Not that we had been stopped. But I felt the pressure of their presence. I thought about the jellyfish befouling our mechanics. Why hadn't

Hurston ordered the ship to go around the island? I didn't ask him.

"They have no brain," Rita said. "It seems they've been as they are now for half a billion years. Fish are only three hundred fifty, less than four hundred million years old. Jellyfish react to stimuli, light, heat, cold. They have a mouth that also serves as the anus." I expected Rita to follow that with a sarcasm, but she didn't. She just added, "They can regenerate themselves if they get a chunk bitten out.

"I said they thrive in our pollution. Carbonic acid, from the burning of carbon based fuels, is deadly to marine life— dissolves shells, stunts coral reefs, but when they put jellyfish in water that is even more acidic than we have now they reproduce more than they do now. The same with the rise in temperature."

The mass of the creature-island made a sloshing noise against the ship.

"You can," Rita went on, "eat some species. Some protein, few calories. Great diet food."

Rory broke in. "I've tasted them—in Japan. Cut in strips and dried." We looked to him for the verdict. "Someone at my table—a gourmet, of course, said it was like squid. I thought it was a stringy, unpalatable seaweed: salty rubber bands. Maybe undried jellyfish would be more like a pudding," he joked.

Hurston, who had taken all this in silently, said, "When I was maybe twenty—southern California, I was taking a long swim—ran into a stretch of them when I was far from shore. I was going diagonally across a bay. It was just as far to go back to shore as to go ahead. Must've been a quarter of a mile of jellyfish. I was stung from my neck to my ankles. When I finally got out I was red. But I had this rush of adrenaline. I was pumped up from the stings."

"Want to swim that now?" said Rita, smiling.

Hurston gave his own smile. "It's one of those experiences you need only once. Let's just hope they don't do something to the ship."

But he seemed to say this as a matter of form, not true worry. *The Argus* passed through the jellyfish island unharmed. Though all of us were made sombre by this short, labored passage. Later I watched Blaise's footage. I saw what I hadn't noted when in the midst of the jellyfish island: plastic debris. The bits and pieces of our creations bobbing about the jellyfish—or blending into their mass. And there seemed to me then some sort of relation of the plastic debris to the innumerable jellies, a feeling I really could not clarify later.

16.

We came nearer to the center of the Patch. Hurston, Rita and Rory were busy with their various aspects of the mission; essentially Hurston went from one to the other, apparently trying to mingle fact and theory that would aid in the beginning of some Grand Plan to reverse, to end the plague of all this techno trash upon the waters. Melissa complained that there wasn't much to report on: dead fish and jellyfish. "Got a shot of one, that's all you need."

If jellyfish thrived in our pollutions, we did now see a fair number of them dead, probably, like the fish, from ingesting minute amounts of plastic—though we did see more alive than not, if no further jellyfish islands.

While Blaise seemed pleased at inactivity and Melissa's frustration, I found Emile and Jorges preternaturally silent, occupied with the functioning of the ship, resigned to a dullness they had perhaps first known as harbor bound workers in the Hamptons. One day I saw Jorges give one of the Buddhas that still lingered on deck a casual kick. Jorges laughed quietly as the plastic image of Nirvana's top man toppled over and bounced without much sound. I had privately begun to call the remaining Buddhas "the sacred cows"; I had no name for the mannequin, that still pointed us in our direction. In fact, I had become so used to it being there, that I hardly noted it at all.

Then one mid-morning Hurston announced we were in the very center of the Great Pacific Garbage Patch. The water was dead calm, more torporous than ever, the sky utterly blue and the sun furious with its light and heat. I thought, as if in vague antidote, of Hurston's surreal artic adventure. There was no more indication that we were at the center of the Patch than someone standing at the center of either pole would discern that fact. I was trying to feel some sense of climax; but it seemed I was just *here*, in the midst of a dead sea. I could see no evidence of plastic garbage, of garbage of any kind about the ship, though here and there was the glint of some dead marine life, evidence that the techno trash, like a pathogen too minute for our vision, worked its virulence.

In what has been a lifelong tendency to the proclivity of a Doubting Thomas, I said to Hurston, "This is the *exact* center?"

"Maybe a hundred yards either way."

"There isn't a variation—the size, the circumference? I would think the weather—"

He replied as if bored with a question that couldn't matter. "It seems to stay pretty regular."

"You mean like the Red Spot on Jupiter?"

He seemed disconcerted I would match his *bête noire* with that celestial anomaly. "I guess like that," he said.

Looking over the water, from horizon to horizon, perhaps

perversely trying to see some tangible bit of trash, I wondered how does the "weather' on Jupiter stay so consistent as to keep the vortex of the atmosphere in that spot constant for the hundreds of years we have been spying it through our optics? We think of weather as changeable, but maybe we as a civilization have not seen the Great Red Spot long enough to know its seasons.

Rita had heard my remark about the Red Spot and later said to me, "Actually it *is* changing. Not so long ago you could fit three Earths in it; now it's just a little more than one. But NASA says as it's shrinking it's growing taller—I guess becoming more cylindrical than oblate."

I said, "That's it. Disappoint me. No constants in the universe."

"Physics, yes; the rest no. In fact, Saturn's rings will probably disappear in a hundred million years or so."

"What have I got to look forward to? Think there'll still be people on Earth then? Humans anywhere at all?"

Rita smiled. "If 'we' are around then, we will be so different that we here now would not recognize 'us' at all.'

*   *   *

Rory was happy, in a quiet, now-I-can-get-to-work-way, finding threads of plastic in the water and twice calling me over to his microscope to see even smaller threads.

"Did you find your plastic DNA?" I asked.

"Still so much to analyze. I don't think I'll exactly *see* it…." His eye returned to the lens, shutting out the larger, outer world.

On deck I approached Emile and Jorges, who seemed to be having a conversation they didn't want anyone to hear. They fell suddenly silent.

"Well," I said, "we're half way to going back."

Emile gave a false smile and said something brief in Spanish. I added, "Maybe you'll be able to say—ten years from now—you were on an historic voyage—"

What was I babbling? They looked at me as if thinking that, too. Jorges looked away, to the ocean. "I don't like this. It's too dead."

The three of us looked over the endless water that ran with monotony to the horizon. In fact, both sea and sky seemed of the same ilk—immemorial, inhuman, and vast: relentless in their merged being. (Or would the existentialists say "nonbeing"?) Anyway, I think I also sensed—was stricken by—the immanence alongside, which not so much mocked human effort but rendered it worthless. If the waters were so fouled with the virus of human debris, with the minute byproducts of our careless civilization, it was all, yes, indeed minute, this mark of ours. Even as our trash corded the planet, violated land and water, the Earth could dwarf and outlast this illness. Like the sickness we feel from the toxins of bacteria the immune system killed, an illness that would be ultimately sloughed off, the Earth bore the illness of us, which it would outlast. For on that sea, beneath that sky, in the timelessness of that day, I felt so palpably that Existence that exists past us, actually apart from and beyond us, and which we touch only in apprehending it, not shaping it. At least not yet....

*　　*　　*

At the end of the second day floating in the calm, Rory asked Emile and Jorges to help him raise up some gelatinous mass of plastic that was virtually invisible even when looking right down upon it from the edge of the ship. Imagine a plastic fishing net made that had been degraded into a transparent gooiness—as if some giant jellyfish had been filtered into a perforated sheet. Perhaps this was the ultimate end of all those fishing nets. Rory had hooked part of it, and raised it from the surface of the water to the level of his shoulders; it stretched in an unpleasant thinness that the preoccupied scientist found a happy enough occurrence to yell out in the way of a boy who had stumbled upon a wonderful toy, or game.

I was nearby, and, looking at this I thought—as I had often thought on this voyage—that here was another bit of the strange: the unnatural. Rory looked as if he were pulling the flesh of some elastic creature from the water, a creature so foreign to our life that Rory's tug and grasp could hardly affect it. He was like an ant bending a hair on a giant's chest. And he knew he was into something large. He extended a portion of what he grasped to Emile by keeping one hand clutched on the plastic jelly and running his other hand along the substance to stretch it out laterally. Emile, with a repulsed look, grasped this weird offering with both hands and tugged, stepping backwards—but Rory exhorted him to do as he did: hold a bit of it in one hand, then draw up more by stretching out the other hand lengthwise. Both men did this in a sort of rough harmony for almost half a minute, as more of the—I almost said "creature"—mass came up out of the water, but a sudden swell of the ocean (not a big swell, a small one) disturbed the tension between the stretch of the plastic jelly and the men. They stumbled backward, then were jerked forward. Perhaps because he was more being commanded than following his own direction, Emile lurched far forward, and was yanked overboard.

There was a simultaneous cry from both Jorges and Rory. Emile went under, then shot up to the surface, struggling—it was instantly plain he was tangled in the mass—that abruptly slapped at and closed over him, almost invisibly. The eye caught only a shimmering of light, points of darting reflection.

Emile was struggling, trying to swim, crying out, going under—

Rory dove into the water. I cried out at his plunge: a great "No!" What saved the scientist was that the mass, at the point of Emile's weight, had apparently wrapped all of itself about his body. So Rory dove into free, clear water. Though as he stroked the short distance to Emile, he too probably would have been caught by the plastic quicksand mass if it had not entirely, it seemed, wrapped about Emile—and sunk, with a horrifying quickness.

Rory, and in another instant Hurston, were swimming above the spot where Emile had gone down. Bravely they dove repeatedly into the turgid ocean. They were spared Emile's fate. Soon they clambered onto the lifeboat Blaise had lowered—with an alacrity that had surprised me—and searched for Emile by dragging a net, by diving again, joined by Rita, who had come up on deck and at my blurted words relating what had happened ("Caught—in some plastic thing!"), had also plunged into the water. Melissa and I, as if for the moment in the stereotypical role of helpless females, called out in horrified astonishment from the deck.

Well, I was no great swimmer, and certainly I wasn't going to be diving into that mass of plasticine marine quicksand.

But what was Jorges doing? His companion, his countryman, his fellow worker going back to the duties inflicted by the nouveau riche of the Hamptons, had been swallowed by some inanimate monster and the indifferent sea, but he was not out there, searching and diving, but looking on this with the same pinned horror as Melissa and myself, uttering fragments in Spanish and English—one of which was the pathetic—and true, no doubt: "I can't swim! I can't swim!" It was an involuntary declaration of his helplessness, his helplessness amidst all this as a whole, this voyage, his life as a menial laborer in a country or countries not his own, his labor for foreigners—

There was a great cry from Hurston on the lifeboat, an anguished bellow: a man-beast throwing back his head and shouting out a cry of defeat. And though he and Rory and Rita and even Blaise returned to their efforts of diving, of dragging the net, Hurston's bellow marked for me the realization that Emile was lost: drowned; dead.

*   *   *

We spent the rest of the day searching in ever widening circles for Emile. I went out with Rita, and even Melissa, who, I think, was as honestly horrified as the rest of us, though she directed Blaise to scan the ocean with his camera, a shot of ocean that could have been taken in many places at many times and could be in the midst of the Patch or on the other side of the world. Though we did see—or thought we saw—something that marked this as the Patch: glimmerings of light, more than the sun off the water, glimmerings as if of that jellyfish plastic in this distance or that, upon or just below the surface of the water. But it was a quick indefinite glimmering; we couldn't be sure….

This incident was the ultimate "strangeness" to the voyage that made each of us feel—I'm sure of this—*The Argus'* mission had been thoroughly mocked and twisted by an ugly roll of fate—or some word we couldn't know, some force we couldn't name. That night Hurston duly—as if he had to torture himself with the duty—tapped out the details of Emile's death on his log, the black letters appearing in terrible precision on the laptop's bright screen. Rory and I, beside him, were quiet, very quiet. When Hurston finished, he turned to us. "Do we just—go back? Go on?" This was unusual for him—to ask directions.

Neither of us answered. As far as I knew, Hurston had not decided from the very beginning, when we'd left San Francisco, if *The Argus* would cross the Patch, to Asia, or just go to the center of the Patch and turn back; or go to the other end of the Patch, turn back….

"There's still more work to do," Rory said, softly. "It's awful to even think of anything else now, but—"

Hurston wasn't looking at us. He was looking downward at some inner depth, some abyss: "Yes, there's always work…." As if he now looked upon work as having terrible aspects. And then, as if feeling he had to add *something*: "We've seen a lot—"

He didn't have to add words to that: we certainly had.

Still softly, but firmly, Rory said, "We went through so much before we got here. We need to stay in the center a little longer. To find—"

"A giant plastic jellyfish?" Hurston shot back, looking fully at Rory now.

Rory didn't back down. "Whatever you want to call it. We've got to know the extent of—this." He gestured behind him.

He stopped when Hurston let out a tangled gush of air. "I need to—it's not exactly mourn. I'm just…shocked." Then, in a diversion of pique, he said, more to himself than anyone: "I want Rita to get that ugly thing off—off my ship."

It was understandable. You can tolerate weirdness if things aren't too ugly. But once something like this has happened, you don't want a weather-worn mannequin with battered face and body pointing the way of the ship.

"I'll tell her," I said.

"*I'll* tell her," he said. To Rory, Hurston said, "A little longer. Yeah, study that—like something out of a stupid horror move. The Loch Ness Monster of the Patch."

Rory replied carefully. "I'll see what I can find."

Hurston nodded, glumly. He went back to the laptop. Facing the screen, he said to us as he typed, "How long does it take a drowned body to surface?"

I looked at Rory. His face had no expression. I was thinking about what he had said about replicating plastic DNA: a reproducing polymer. And Hurston's: "…a stupid horror movie."

Rory continued not to note my stare; or, if he did, he did not care.

*   *   *

That evening I was on deck. The moon, nearly full, was out. It silvered the water. Were any of the glimmerings on the night-time water of the plastic "thing"?

I wasn't the only one thinking those thoughts. Melissa, bearing an expression I'd never seen, joined me. "That—whatever it was—could be right out there. How…ugly. Garbage—plastic—" She shook her head. "Unnatural."

I should have murmured some assent, but instead I said, "Is that how you said it for the documentary? Unnatural?"

She sighed. "I'm too tired. Don't mock me."

"I wasn't," I half lied.

"Look, I've covered wars. Afghanistan, Iraq. But this. Like something—like when Hurston was telling that story—out of Poe."

"Horror movie, he said, today."

We were quiet. Then she said, nodding to the sea, "How long does it take?"

"I don't know."

"I don't want to be around when he comes up. I almost hope we don't find him. Of course, it would decent that we…."

"The dead. Just like war."

"Stop. Just stop. You in your ivory tower. Or is it ivy?"

I shrugged. I let a pause grow before saying, "I'm not in any tower."

"Oh, you are. Science."

"There's something wrong—with science?"

"I certainly don't know much science. But I know it can be just as much of a game as—what I do."

These were thoughts I'd had on this voyage—and before. "So we both—do games?"

"The games are the real things of life. All we've got."

We stared at each other a bit, said nothing further, and looked seaward again. There were other glimmerings on the water: moonlight on the dead bodies of fish—slain, like Emile, by plastic.

17.

The next morning, we had a memorial service for Emile. Hurston had a small black book that he opened with the air of "I guess I have to do this—" Not that he resented a duty, but wasn't sure he was up to bearing it. He pursed his lips with deliberation, squinting in the hot light (the way he had when we pulled out of San Francisco), not trusting what he might say would be adequate. A sound came from him; he stopped. He held up the book, gave an expression that said, "Isn't this ridiculous—inadequate?—then spoke whatever words came to him.

"Emile, along with Jorges, have worked with me…well before this voyage. And I know both worked together—"

We stood in a rough circle before Hurston, though Jorges stood a little out of this approximate circumference. I thought

Hurston's linking Jorges to Emile right at the beginning gave the uncomfortable flavor that Jorges too was being eulogized.

Not that it was exactly a eulogy. Hurston really knew little of Emile's life. Perhaps Jorges should have come forward and said something, but none of us expected that, and Jorges did not. I sensed it would be too awkward for him to talk about his feelings, his memories of his countryman, with foreigners. He remained with bowed head as Hurston spoke in generalizations about life on the sea—sincere generalizations, actually. "—It can be a clear pure world, but you always know…it's an element we came upon." (That recalled something he had said at the end of his artic story.) "We don't live here, we pass over it." You could mark that as a symbol for life itself—which we pass through, deluded with our own voyages, until whatever end calls us, expected or not. Without saying it precisely, Hurston spoke of the unexpected. "When something like this— out of, beyond…*experience*—" (what word *could* he use?) "— happens…. You're never prepared. The person it happens to isn't prepared, can't be prepared, and those around that person—the same." Well, that was true, I had to think.

Hurston went on like this. Longer than he should have, I thought. Sincere, but rambling. "I suppose we remember somebody…we only know from a voyage…each in different ways—" Again I was thinking: in life itself we join with others in only parts of their passage. After a moment Hurston added: "He should have stayed with us, still been here." There was silence. Hurston ended with: "We keep him in mind, as we go on." The dead do linger; though the dead of casual association slip to the sides of memory. I'll recall Emile most by the bizarre and horrible way in which he died. And then I was trying to remember if it was Emile or Jorges who had thrown that plastic bottle over the side early on. Oh, yes, it had been

Emile. The violated sea had taken its revenge….

*   *   *

A little while later I was talking to Rory. He was looking out over the waters. "Maybe you think it's sick, but I want to run into that plastic again."

I said, "As long as you don't ask me—anybody—to help you pull it up."

He flashed me a disarming grin. "I'll brave the monster alone. What was that movie—Stephen King's book—*The Shining*. Here, it's 'The Glimmering.'"

He gave a short laugh, continued to look out on the ocean. Then, still looking seaward, he said, "I think what Hurston said about the sea not being our home— Well, he didn't exactly say that, but not our original place. Of course, if you believe in evolution, it's the other way around. We came from—or the beings we came from—came from here, so…. Maybe that's why it draws us. Just think of this: why does a water view beachfront property—why is it more expensive than in the middle of the woods? Something primal: an allure." He turned to smile at me. It was the first time I realized he had a handsome smile. "I'm not being academic. I work in a lab, with plastic, with inanimate things. But I love the beach. I'm a pretty good swimmer."

"I guess you are, the way you were swimming around yesterday."

That was all that we said for awhile. Then, in the distance we both saw—I was about to exclaim even as Rory pointed—a concentrated mass of scattered brilliance: an aggregation of glimmering.

"Is that it?" said Rory quietly.

*   *   *

We moved to it cautiously. Every one of us had a grave face.

Hurston particularly. The area of glimmering grew as we neared—as if we were watching something in the midst of growth; and it did not seem stationary. If there was the usual visual increase in size as we got closer, the glimmering also seemed to expand, as if reaching outward from a central concentration, or rising up from the sea. We were *studying* it, anticipating (the better word) contact with it as if it were alive. Though I believe if any of us had been asked we would have denied that perception. Except maybe Jorges, who muttered phrases, some of which I caught and which meant something to the effect, "Stay back from us."

But we did not give "it" that option. We moved steadily into the mass. Hurston had a look that appeared as if he might burst with the concentration that weighted the course of this action. Was it mad to continue onward?

Blaise had his ubiquitous camera to his eye, Melissa pensively at his shoulder. She was utterly quiet, save for once or twice pointing ahead or to the side and hissing the command, "There!" Blaise would shift his perspective accordingly. But what was there to see, differently? From all angles it was this glimmering, alternating between sharp and dull. And Blaise, it struck me, might have been the one among us, who could express the group's thought simply: he blurted out abruptly: "Does it know we're—here?"

Whether *it* "knew" or not, we were then in it, the glimmering now along our sides, and then behind us as well as in front. Again, as yesterday, *The Argus* slowed; there was the sensation of being caught in some kind of web. Whether that web could literally stay us…. Hurston halted *The Argus* and there we floated, rising just a little now and then with the swell of the torpid sea, beneath the stark cloudless sky, the fierce sun, with the strange plastic mass on and just beneath the water's surface, displaying shards and pricks of light. And in between these points of brilliance, the portion of the morass not involved reflection, a tenuous whitish-grey that seemed of so little substance, a step away from being imagined, from being the ocean's evanescent foam—and yet, because it was part of something so large, and because no part was different than another, there was, on the part of human perception that incomprehensibility (and helplessness) at what appeared to be an infinite redundancy, as we sometimes receive the heavens in venues where artificial lights haven't driven out the stars. As I'd seen the stars from this ship, a view that had its wonder and beauty, but also the indifference of creation.

And then—it was expected: Rory was jabbing alongside the ship, with what looked like a sort of harpoon, a shaft with a hook on the end, and drawing up to the air, the deck, the same sort of substance that had taken Emile and drowned him. I couldn't help stepping back, recoiling. Melissa too stepped back, at the same time demanding Blaise keep filming, and of course he did, half crouched, as if he along with his digital eye were about to capture a moment of violence: of this resolute scientist drawing this Medusa hair from the sea. Rory now held a strand of it that he had plucked from the harpoon and drew it up alongside him, and then above his head. It glimmered, but only a little, much less than it had in the water. Rita stepped forward and touched the Medusa hair, tugged it a little with the stolid reverence of the scientist for what is truly curious and unusual. "Careful!" Hurston barked. Rita didn't release her touch; she looked at him, blinked. "Could this really be dangerous?" her look seemed to say, asking not so much Hurston as herself.

"Something to cut it—!" Rory shot at Rita. In a few seconds Rita had a knife and a small plastic box. Rory now grasped the strand with two hands about three feet apart and Rita cut into the middle of that space, cut through the plastic without much trouble; Rory dropped his severed end from this big mass (how big was it?) into the box, where it fell with an odd sound, not loud but definite, and curled slightly like the piece of a tentacle that had been cut from a giant living creature.

Everyone stared down at it, as if expecting it to move, to twitch. It didn't.

*   *   *

The Argus trudged ahead. "I want to find where the end of this is," said Hurston grimly, a sudden Ahab (hadn't I called him that before?); I made the inevitable (if all too exaggerated) link between the Great White Whale and The Great White Glimmering. The almost supernatural aspect of size and whiteness. But there seemed nothing grand about this plastic mass, only madness. But that was true in *Moby Dick*, too. What's grand about obsessively singling out a certain creature for slaughter?

We tried to reach the edges of the glimmering, but it didn't seem possible. Perhaps the ship's very motion always pushed that edge out before us. Later Rita would say to me, "It was like something I read once: it's impossible to go past the edge of the universe: wherever you are it's there." To be less metaphysical, perhaps that edge was so hard to detect we could not ascertain it. The ship moved slowly, very slowly, apparently impeded by this plastic morass. Rory, in the way of a man making dark mockery out of something very unpleasant, said to Hurston, "Well, there's no center here!"

Hurston shot back, "I said I want the edge!"

But that still eluded *The Argus*. There was no fixed edge to this glimmering. It changed as we moved. We could see, we thought we could see, in the near distance an edge, if not so definite; but, like Zeno's paradox, when we were halfway there we felt we'd made no movement at all. The edge, the indefinite edge, remained just beyond. *This* was a sort of madness, worse than the pursuit of any creature. Well, if not worse morally, than worse to one's perceptions, to the fixed senses that seem the same to us every day. The edgeless, vast glimmering, a brightness of the sea, a brightness that choked not just vision but the throat. The world was too brilliant, too elusive, too oppressive to breathe right. Blaise tilted his head back from his camera—how much of that oppressive monotony had he filmed?—and moaned, loud enough (though softly in a way) for all of us to hear, "It's making me sick." Melissa, in sunglasses, her head darting from horizon to horizon, the horizon that sometimes met the sky with glimmering and sometimes did not—so there was some hope out there—Melissa looked like an eyeless bird, trapped in blackness, her too blonde hair blown about as the glimmering slid over the surface of her dark lenses. There was the sense it hypnotized those hidden eyes.

Rory and Rita seemed the least disturbed. In fact, each seemed engrossed. Rita directed some instrument at various sections of the glimmering; a small black square appeared on the surface of the water. She told me this measured, by contrast, the brightness of reflection of the glimmering. Was this a normal tool for an oceanographer? I didn't ask. Was this plastic jelly supernaturally reflective? I guess Rory would have to answer that. He was wrapt, enwrapt, even enraptured, I thought, by continually hooking some portion of the mass, bringing a strand up to the ship and cutting it himself now, an operation in which he grew rapidly in skill. Some private part of my senses half expected a sound of pain or at least protest from the plastic thing. Though there were a number of strands by him in the box now, glinting a little less as they dried, actually becoming more on the transparent side as they dried— and none twitched or showed any animacy. Though that still did not take away the feeling the glimmering gave us, of the presence of some strange type of life.

To me it felt as if *The Argus* were in a storm of some sort, of strange weather: the climate of a hitherto unknown life. Silently I echoed Blaise: "It's making me sick." The cameraman had given up recording this ugly monotony; his videographic eye dangled by his side. Melissa, with glimmerings on her sunglasses, did not object. Blaise looked out on the brightness, hypnotized, it seemed, or at least pressured into some sort of subjection. Hurston was now a grim, almost waxen-like figure at the wheel of the ship; then suddenly he pointed and shouted—the shout was an instant after the gesture: he had to return his mind to the realm of human words, of which the glimmering was not. He shouted just: "There!" Then again bellowed it: "There!" And we saw *The Argus* before a very definite edge. We were almost out of it; and in a minute or so more it seemed the glimmering had sucked itself right past us and was behind us, where we had been, glimmering in our wake, leaving us like a sated creature who had played cruelly with prey it didn't want (just then), allowing it freedom.

Each of us looked behind us, drained.

18.

I was having a drink with Melissa. She seemed both dazed and annoyed. "I thought this was going to be just some solid help-the-environment-story. It's a Frankenstein saga."

"And who created the monster?"

"Don't make it academic. You know what I mean."

I did, but— "It's just the insanity of people, that's all."

"That's all? I've covered political corruption, child abuse— war. That's the usual insanity. This—"

"That plastic jellyfish is a product of an insanity."

She looked down at her drink. "Things go beyond us," she muttered. It sounded a bit too literate for her—but then, she'd told me that along with Communications she'd majored in English.

Rory was in his glory with his specimens. In his little cabin lab there was segments of what he had severed from the glimmering in all sorts of solutions, beneath the clamps of his microscope, being stretched and twisted by clamps, subjected to the slash of different chemicals, etc. He had the happiness of a researcher in his element. He at once wanted to share some of this with me and saw that my ignorance of his science would slow him down. My visit—intrusion—was short. Rory's brief—but enthusiastic—remarks weren't really illuminating, though I took away the impressions of the severed pieces of the glimmering, none glimmering now, just in various states and hues of grey-white plastic-ness, nondescript and, above all, harmless. But a candle flame seems harmless, until it ignites a conflagration. Not really the most apt analogy, as you can burn a finger by leaving it over the flame for a few seconds, while these pieces of the huge glimmering were ultimately harmless. And to prove it to myself I stuck a finger in one, felt only a drying inanimate softness. Then again, a piece of muscle taken from the body, some brain cells, could hardly intimate the function and power from which they had come.

Though I had to say: "Your plastic life?"

From the microscope Rory gave me a sideways glance. "Not quite. But the way it's been gathered together—" He drew himself away from the scope, looked at me fully. "Would any of us recognize *pre-life*?"

"Maybe Fukushima is working something."

"Like those old Japanese horror movies. Radiation creating—what? There was some old film I saw in college: 1950s B or less than B horror movie festival— Oh, yeah, *The Blob*. Or *Return of the Blob*. Or both. The Blob created by the bomb, nuclear testing."

*   *   *

That afternoon Hurston abruptly unleashed the ugly mannequin from its prominent perch—as Rita watched, not protesting, but smiling, as if the short time she had secured for the simulacrum had been a sufficient statement of sorts. A statement of exactly what, who's to say. Huston gave Rita a glance, then with a sharp breath flung the mannequin out onto the water, the small bit of fishing net that had clung to the side of the face swept free in the air. The mannequin floated in ominous stillness, the damaged face looking up a sky that was slowly filling with thin clouds, weak strips of greyness that blocked the sun only slightly, and did not relieve the heat of the day. By now that face had taken on the inscrutability of an icon. But there was, in me, the irrational hope (which I immediately if unsuccessfully contested) that we were releasing ourselves from the catalyst of a curse. –Or offering a sacrifice to forces we could not understand but which we understood threatened us?

The surreal experiences we had recently undergone, and done so in the isolation of the vast Pacific, had brought out the primitive reality of existence.

It was a while before the mannequin was out of sight. I found myself fixed on its progress, as it drifted away with gradual inexorability, leaving as if with a deliberation that was evidence of a destination—even as I watched for the return of the glimmering.

*   *   *

Perhaps what we dread always comes—as if our dread creates its approach.

The next morning the thin cloud cover of yesterday afternoon had become a sky entirely grey-white. You could see the sun through it, the ghost of a sun, shrouded enough so you could look directly at it.

But the shrouded sun did not lessen its heat, which was oppressive. The sky, sometimes a bit dull, sometimes almost white, was the sort of sky that unsettles you with the sense of a need for caution.

I was on deck with Rita. Apropos of nothing in particular she was rambling on about ocean currents, about "these wheels of water" that churn in oval or elongated regularity about the Earth, remarking on how "The history of exploration depended upon what we try to figure out the science for now—" It was at once a little too scholarly and as if I were listening to some inner dialogue of Rita's, the serious intent of her psyche that was continually disguised by her sardonicism. A little numbed by her discourse, I had perhaps withdrawn into my own interiors, and wasn't really looking outward with enough attention when Rita suddenly blurted out "Look!" pointing to the horizon. It took a moment to refocus my attention.

I saw a form floating on the waters; and, around it, the faintest glimmering.

It was a darker glimmering now, and the form it carried was the mannequin, returned—as I saw clearly in the binoculars Rita passed to me. But even as I ascertained that, I gasped as I made out another body, just beyond the mannequin.

"Emile?" I said, with utter dismay, as I lowered the

binoculars and Rita took them quickly.

In the dull glimmering both forms came toward us; along with, if you could call it a form, the glimmering, almost imperceptible in the unbrilliant light. Rita and I stood there, disconcerted—shocked?—each in a different way. Eventually I called the others. We lined the railing of the ship as first the mannequin, then Emile, drew into closer vision: Emile, his body bloated with his death (as though death had expanded his body rather than diminished it), his enfattened face with opened eyes staring grotesquely into that dull, whitened sky. His corpse had an unpleasant sheen, as if with the slime of the glimmering; here and there were the more tangible strands of fishing nets trailing from him, stretching past him in the water. And as the dull glimmering lapped at the ship, we drew poor Emile up from the water, netted him like a great sad fish. Hurston looked upon the drowned man with such clear anguish I felt more sorry for the living man than the dead one. Emile lay there, dripping water from his sodden clothes and bloated flesh, and we all stared down at this man whom we'd memorialized—was it only yesterday?

Suddenly Hurston shouted over his shoulder "Leave it!" as he saw Rory and Rita raising what he thought to be the mannequin from the water; but Rory turned and said quite calmly, "Just getting some more samples." Even at that moment the scientist reigned: as if it were irrational to invest further emotion in this man's death. Rory drew up more strands of the glimmering and Rita helped him cut them. Apparently, she had no inclination of retrieving her mannequin. Or judged, quite rightly, it would not be the moment to do so.

Soon the mannequin floated past us, borne by the currents Rita could so meticulously describe. It was as if it had left us to retrieve our dead, and now, that done, could easily depart.

Or was it borne by the glimmering? There was a thought: could the glimmering move *apart* from the current?

*   *   *

So now we had a second service for Emile—his body making it a more definite one, of course, but the fact that it was the second in as many days made it seem more bizarre (I'm using that word a lot, I know) than sorrowful. Not that it wasn't sad. The body, wrapped in a weighted dark plastic tarpaulin, a more solid plastic than any shards of fishing nets or glimmering. This dark, tight, heavy shroud seemed at once a poignant and pathetic end-of-life mass that mocked the very promise of life, mocked any extent of innocence, wisdom, kindness that any one life could have possessed.

Hurston stood by the plastic-shrouded body. Hard put to go through this a second time, he said, "We consigned you to your life's end without you visible here before us. Now, that we *see*…." He faltered. His eyes held tears. He began again: "Now that we see—you…it is no different—" (Yet it was, in some way I couldn't explain.) "The body seen, the body unseen—when death is *known*—" Some inner vision was causing him to find a poetry that wasn't literally explainable with words. "We do not need the proof of your presence; we knew your presence gone yesterday. Ours is the task to give your body to the sea again—the body that is now the remnant but not the self we knew—"

My God. It was giving me chills. Never mind that neither Hurston nor any of us (save Jorges) really "knew" Emile. Hurston, his face drawn with tragedy, was giving us a eulogy for everyman.

"To whatever realm you have already gone—whatever place of which we can't conceive—" I looked at Hurston, his aspect caught in something that hardly seemed himself: *he* was in another realm: "…you have our prayers…." He said that last word not as cliché but as acknowledgment that we possess some possibility of spiritual urgency that reaches through the dregs of sorrow.

There was a long silence. Jorges, again standing apart, seemed more stricken with disbelief than anguish. In that anguish was an enormous sense of isolation.

He held his apartness as Hurston, Rory and Blaise raised the darkly covered body, staggered with it a moment, raised it above the ship's railing, then flung it over. Perhaps Jorges did not want to touch the death of someone who had come from his own "realm"—death might then become familiar to him, too.

The body of Emile hit the torpid sea with a preternatural splash, and slowly sank. Blaise and I watched that spot of water until there was no sign it had been disturbed. When my eyes looked elsewhere, out to the far sea, I thought I saw the faintest glimmering, but I half believed it imagination. The day and the sky had remained fouled with oppressive grey-white light.

We scattered to our cabins, save for Rita, who walked the deck slowly, in circuits of introspection. As vocal and brilliant as Rita was, it was always hard to figure what went on in her mind. Perhaps, along with the horror of Emile's end, she thought of her mannequin, now drifting in the distance, like a mocking image of the human being we had let the sea reclaim.

*   *   *

Below, Melissa—maybe just to distract herself from all this sorrowful strangeness—was saying to Blaise, "We should've brought him back. So his family—"

"And how," cut in Rory, "would we have preserved him? We don't have the facilities for…a morgue. Unless you want to empty our refrigerator and—"

Blaise's voice was of someone who had been abruptly

pushed to a limit: "Please, please! Can't we let it go!"

I was suddenly struck with something very surprising. Melissa had not had that second service for Emile filmed. Perhaps even she had been exhausted by the events of the voyage, and her modern insistence of recording everything had finally been confounded by an event she did not wish to visually replay. Or, even more: had annihilated the very thought of a desire to record—returning her senses to an older view (if briefly), that an event like this happens once and is not to be *seen* again, only retold. (What had Hurston exactly meant about 'seeing'?) Melissa, as all of us, would replay the second service of Emile, the casting of his body into the sea privately, each in his or her own way—as it should be.

Melissa threw up her hands at Blaise's plea, said nothing.

And none of us mentioned it the rest of the day. Or the next. Jorges went about his duties like a man sentenced to activities from which something deadly might spring at him at any moment.

Meanwhile, *The Argus* floated on. The next day was bright again, and Rita and Rory gathered some more minute, even microscopic samples of degraded debris from the sea. Though the plastics man was more fixed on what he had gleaned from the glimmering.

He gave me an update that sunk into technicalities too often for me to follow as closely as I would have liked, but he did say he was seeing "evidence" that the plastic "here was on the verge of interacting with the sea water into the *possibility* of a *sort* of replication." His face was earnest, insisting I accept this "possibility." I listened, yet this seemed a conclusion—if you could call it a conclusion—that was too fraught with the speculation of his own desires—for a transformation to happen that was more science fictional than nonfictional. Actually, he sounded a little crazy to me. I suppose the discovery of a plastic DNA-type replication was Nobel material…. Though it wasn't that I thought Rory was addicted to any desire for household fame—which I had seen in more than a few scientists. He was in it for the wonder of it, and what he sought would be wondrous indeed. Or would it? If a type of plastic "reproduction" occurred, would the oceans be filled with huge flotillas of glimmerings? Ocean Earth taken over by a huge mass of plastic glimmerings? True plastic islands? Plastic continents? I said something of that sort to Rory. He regarded me in a way that showed he thought about it seriously.

"I couldn't say. Would conditions be *that* favorable for that? Especially if we contain this trash? As I'm sure we will—" (Scientists are often optimists.) "I really can't see Frankenstein plastic jelly monsters proliferating—"

Though maybe I could. I said, "Let me ask you this. If left alone, the way things are now, could there be—if all your possibilities came true—an *evolution*—in time—of a plastic-based animate life?" I was getting on his ride, seeing how he reacted.

"Well…." He looked toward his microscope, beneath whose lens was clamped a minute piece of the glimmering. "Though, based on our definitions…I'm not sure if many would call it *life*—"

"…*our* definitions." But he wasn't speaking of *his* definitions.

We might have gone deep into an interesting if esoteric conversation about just what constitutes "life," when Rita came in and said, with a perplexed sort of worry, "Our captain has something important to tell us, it seems."

"What?" I asked.

"I don't know. He wants everyone in his cabin."

19.

We gathered before Hurston in the tight small space. There was the crackle of the radio, the hiss of air spaces without voice—but he told us there had been a voice: "Langhorn—I got this broken transmission—he said...'*pirates*.' They killed Fukara, took his ship. Destroyed a lot of Smith's operations—ravaged the islands—"

Blaise: "Oh, my God, I'm starting to believe in curses."

Rory: "Are you sure—pirates?"

Rita: "Is he—Langhorn—Smith—all right? Did they—any of the others—?"

Melissa was as surprisingly silent as Jorges—who literally crossed himself, something I'd seen him do at both our ceremonies for Emile. These exclamations, silences and involuntary protections came out more or less at once. Hurston made a gesture that expressed his own shock and a plea to let him continue.

"I've been trying to get him again, but I haven't—yet. He said they killed more than Fukara. I don't know how many. I don't know if it was all on that—that ship—they took—"

"*The Gatherer*," said Rita.

"Yes." He looked at her as if with annoyance. "Langhorn said—I wasn't sure, too much static—a lot of sunspots right now—Smith was roughed up—but alive—and something about supplies being taken—"

Blaise asked, "Where'd these pirates come from?"

"Somalia?" I offered, stupidly.

"That's another ocean," Hurston snapped. "He didn't say where. Something about—no, he did say—Asian. He thought Chinese. And then he said—I think—an African—"

Rory: "That's confusing. Were you able to talk with him?"

"A little. He said he had a problem hearing me. Maybe it was worse on his end."

Rita said flatly: "We have to go back there."

Rory: "Shouldn't the Coast Guard—?"

Rita snapped at him. "The Coast Guard isn't in the middle of the Pacific. We're thousands of miles from America." She said to Hurston, "The pirates are still there?"

Hurston exhaled in frustration—and fear? "I'm not sure. It seemed—he was talking as if—they'd just left—come in, destroyed everything and left—"

Rita: "We have any weapons?"

"There's that one rifle I never use."

"You know how to use it?"

Apparently Hurston took this as a challenge. "If I have to."

"I guess that's something," said Rita dismissively. "I've never fired anything." She looked at the rest of us. None offered any martial experience.

Hurston spoke firmly. "Yes, we're going back."

Melissa finally spoke. "Can we get in touch with anyone? A UN force?"

Hurston: "We're in the middle of the ocean. It would be a while before anyone—" He broke off and said, as if to himself, "He sounded pretty bad. Like somebody…broken."

I guessed that to be an accurate word. Langhorn had always seemed to me to be a man full of stretched nerves.

Melissa said, "Captain" (it was so natural to say, but she had never addressed Hurston like that before) "we could be going into something that…."

Hurston: "Could get us all killed."

"You heard, there's already been murder."

"Something like that." As if he wanted to make murder

vague. He added. "It'll be a great denouement for your—your film."

Melissa: "Am *I* creating this—all this madness.?"

Hurston: "This environmental voyage is already screwed. Unfortunately, we've got to go."

Blaise said to Rory, "Can I pet one of your Buddha heads?"

"Might not be a bad idea," said the plastics man, shrugging at this next chapter of the absurd, and not caring if perhaps he were being mocked.

* * *

Within minutes, literally, we were on our way back to the plastic islands, leaving the torpid waters of the center of the Great Pacific Garbage Patch, sightings of dead marine life— and, yes, the glimmering. Which, as if this were a movie, appeared once more, not surrounding us as it had before, but whose understated edge ominously lapped at our port side, making us aware of its reach and expanse—that ran, roughly sparkling in this bright day, to the horizon. Jorges, between his duties, crossed himself again, and Rory, as could only be expected, jabbed at the sea for some samples. But for the most part this edge of the glimmering was elusive; Rory brought up a strand or two and Rita, as before, cut some pieces for further study, though the oceanographer was plainly annoyed, obviously feeling there was something more pressing to consider. Blaise dutifully recorded Rory and Rita and the stretch of the glimmering for what would certainly be the most bizarre (yes, that word) environmental documentary. Bizarre that we were taking samples of the bizarre while on something that might be called a rescue mission. Or suicide mission?

Hurston offered this terse comment as he briefly joined me on deck: "Like we're leaving something that knows us. But we don't know it." Then he returned below to try the radio again.

But all the while back to the plastic islands Langhorn—or anyone else—could not be raised.

*   *   *

There was an inevitable—inexorable?—surrealness to our return: The appearance again of large plastic debris, the heat and light of the endless ocean. We talked among ourselves in starts, like bursts of desperate conversation erupted from silence. I think all of us, each of us, were afraid, but bound. Even Melissa, whom I would always assess as the most self-centered among us. That first evening heading back I looked over the shoulder of the newswoman and Blaise as they reviewed footage of the voyage. ("Rough cut," said Blaise, as if bringing me into the process of his profession). I saw too much of myself in this video record, even though I was usually just in the background; my documented presence, which seemed too casually and sporadically produced, made me uncomfortable; I was not at all pleased with my image, which was now virtually immortal. But more than this, it was too much for me to see all this again, to see—everything. From the prosaic debris to Emile's body riding the glimmering. In between the mannequin and the Buddhas there were shots of Rory like a mad harpooner bringing up strands of that almost animate plastic.... Melissa suddenly drew back and exclaimed, "Who can see all this and be sane?" She said it poignantly, with feeling: sincere. Blaise looked at her—without the surprise I would have expected, as if he had known (or sensed) this side of her—and turned back, without comment to scenes of the plastic islands, of Arturo Smith gesturing to the stretch of the archipelago, the incomplete ziggurat, the giant face of computer monitors—

It *was* too much. I went out on the deck, to look at the stars, but checked myself from intruding—I felt it would be that—

on Rita and Hurston by the railing, bent towards each other in low conversation.

As I've said, I had felt Hurston both particularly annoyed at Rita's continual sardonicism and attracted to her. Had Blaise filmed naked Rita before the Buddha? I couldn't remember. What Rita thought of our captain beyond her sardonic perspective, I wasn't sure. But now there seemed a peaceful, untroubled comradeship... Well, maybe it was a truce—or a case of surrender, an acceptance of forever being at odds, a necessary closing of ranks before whatever awaited us at the plastic islands. I tried to discern something more definite in the cast of the silhouettes of their heads, but could not. I retreated below.

In my cabin I heard an indistinct murmuring. I listened and listened and could barely make out the cadence of what seemed like a prayer in Spanish from Jorges, of course, drifting through the body of the ship. I am not one to pray, believing that the Being—the Force—whatever—who had wrought all this was *not* one to note the fall of every sparrow. It would have been a comfort to believe in beseeching, but I didn't. The universe I lived in exhibited a continual, random indifference. And I *was afraid*, this night, in the peaceful dark, as we headed toward...danger. Even if it turned out to be an aftermath of danger, I knew there would be something shattering about it.

20.

Just before we reached Smith's archipelago a mist of fog came (what is the difference between mist and fog?) upon the sea. In the bright day there hung ahead of us a twisting shroud of grey. It seemed ominous. *The Argus* entered it slowly. It would be an exaggeration to say it blotted out all light, that we could barely see ahead of us, but the greyness certainly cut vision in half and gave everything the cast of, if not quite a dream, an aspect that caused me at last to say, "Am I seeing what I'm seeing?"

It was. We were. The archipelago, the main flat plastic island—Gilligan's Island—gave both blatant and subtle evidence of some sort of damage. On that big island there was the smoky remnant of some fire rising from the edge (the "shoreline"), with the unpleasant smell of burning plastic. The island that had been the base of the giant computer monitor face was half ravaged, so that this weirdly modernistic visage now looked even more like something from an apocalypse. An island meant to be a skyline showed silhouettes of "buildings" that had been truncated. And on these islands scattered figures, color-dimmed in the mist, moved—as if with a sort of hesitation, as if questioning their own movement as well as our approach. But however eerie all this was, and certainly foreboding, I think all of us felt the relief that it seemed no actual danger was awaiting us.

This was the case. We were not so much greeted as approached as we docked. Several of Smith's workers drifted to an uncertain distance before us, then halted—though surely not expecting danger from us. They looked not so much physically as emotionally battered; their eyes held the aspect of people who had witnessed—something. Not one of them spoke to us in those first moments—and then there was the sharp cry, a cry coming closer, a figure half running, half walking, towards us, another dull wraith of the mist, but a vocal one: Langhorn. He was decidedly thinner; his shirt and shorts were ripped and dirty. And dirt and sweat had dried on his face.

"Oh, my God, I'm so glad—"

Hurston said to him—with a curt efficiency that was meant

to be a manly manner of not commenting on his appearance: "You're all right?"

Langhorn stopped before us, breathing hard, his eyes settled into a sort of relief and a sort of calm. "They're gone. They're gone. Most of us—OK—"

It was Melissa who asked: "Where's Smith?"

Langhorn's face lost a little of its relief. He gestured behind us. "He's—he's—hurt. They roughed him up. He—he—protested—crazy—brave—you wouldn't think…. They pointed guns at him—could've shot him—he wouldn't shut up. They *beat him*—" His voice collapsed in empathy with those last words, as if Langhorn had just now realized the injury that had been done to Smith.

Rory broke in: "You said they killed—"

"Fukara. Three others." He shot this out with a painful breath. He looked past us, to the horizon obscured by greyness. "Threw them into the water. Out there with the trash—"

As if she was doing an on-the-air interview, Melissa asked, "What exactly happened?"

Langhorn looked at her worriedly. It seemed he didn't want to go into further details right then. He abruptly said to Hurston, "We all have to get away from here."

"I've put a call out to international channels. I'm sure soon—"

I couldn't tell if that satisfied Langhorn or not. He brushed some hair back from his forehead. "Smith'll want to see you." And just like that we were following him. And just like that there was a change in his manner. He had taken Smith to task before; now he seemed intent on aiding him. Anyway, there was a desperate benevolence to it.

Further into the interior of Gilligan's Island were the plastic living quarters, and in one plastic hut, that had the smell of burnt plastic about it, was Smith, half reclining on a dirty mattress, his face a collage of bruises, his clothes tattered. He started as we came in, there was fear on his face—Langhorn had been calling out "Arturo! Arturo!" before we entered, before the beleaguered conceptual artist knew what was coming upon him, more calamity or rescue. It could have meant the return of the pirates, the return of *their* rough ugly brand of conceptual art. In that first instant when I saw Arturo Smith again, happy Bohemian and forerunner of art too large for a museum to contain, the creator of works whose size alone put them in another category, in which size was part of their very art and definition—I saw Arturo Smith had been grossly invaded by the cruel world, his work despoiled, his psyche surely upheaved. Not only had his works been vandalized, his supplier had been murdered—an act that said, *You could be next.* An act that indicated the devil could reach to at least the periphery of Smith's soul.

Rita, as if she were a nurse, knelt beside Smith and began to softly press against his face, his neck, his arms and ask him gently, "Are you hurt very badly?" And "Does this hurt? Does this—?" In a way that might have aroused a man that hadn't been battered. Smith accepted her touch with a glad weariness. Kindness had returned to the world.

Melissa, not at all in her interviewer's voice, said, "Can you talk, Arturo?"

He nodded, but did not speak.

A bit more professionally, Melissa asked again, "What exactly happened?"

Smith looked to Langhorn who looked back. Smith led off; Langhorn jumped in here and there, retreated; sometimes both spoke over each other, interweaving events with different perspectives, giving us a story that was surprising it had happened in the first place but not surprising that, once it had happened, had happened in this way.

Smith said, "Alfredo, on the ziggurat, he saw the ship first. We tried to contact them. Fukara was nervous—I always knew he did more than I knew about. I didn't think he was worried about bringing me some plastic—" Smith took in a breath, touched the side of his face, gingerly probing a soreness. Rita still crouched by him, but leaned back a little. For some reason I thought of her naked on the deck, by the Buddhas.

Langhorn said, "It's as if Fukara knew what it would be. It was a ship without any markings—ugly, battered, big. Dark—black. It couldn't've looked more ominous. Arturo was asking me if I had called in some visitors—" He gave the artist a wry look. "I think we were all—apprehensive." He said that last word as if mocking that earlier perspective; events would prove any anxiety euphemistic to what followed.

At any rate, anxiety warped perception. "The ship seemed to come on faster—there seemed something unreal about it—impossible—a speeded up dream. Before they reached us there were shots—shots, explosions—I felt something bursting somewhere on the island. They reached us, just poured out. But we were done before they even set foot—"

Smith cut in sharply. "You're sounding hysterical."

Langhorn cringed. "I'm trying—why don't *you* just give the facts." He gave the last word mockery, as if facts had been hard to pin down in that situation.

Smith did give the facts, as he had seen them. Slowly, with the tiredness of an injured man, who now works with the psyche that the world easily reaches out to batter. The strange ship had docked right alongside *The Gatherer*; men tumbled out from the ship onto both *The Gatherer* and the plastic island. "A crowd. You wouldn't think—" started Langhorn. Smith cut him off again, saying prosaically, "There were a lot of them. It happened fast. I think they killed Fukara right away. I don't know if he...resisted them at all—I mean, I don't how he *could have* resisted them."

Hurston asked both Langhorn and Smith, "You said they were Asian?"

Langhorn: "I think Chinese. All except—an African. I'm not sure if he was in charge, but he seemed—"

Smith: "He was. He gave the orders. In their language."

Hurston: "A Chinese-speaking African leading Chinese pirates?"

Smith closed his eyes and appeared to ponder a wave of pain. "Why not?"

Indeed, for a man floating on a plastic island of his creation in the midst of the Pacific, why not? All events can be allowed to be strange—bizarre.

In the continuing alternation between Langhorn and Smith, we heard the rest of the story; or at least the portion of the story the two had witnessed: the pirates swarming over both Fukara's ship and Gilligan's Island— "You wouldn't've thought that ship could hold so many," said Smith, echoing an impression which we had just heard Langhorn expressing. "The strangest thing," said Langhorn, "the way it strikes me now, they had the look of Chinese musicians in an orchestra, practiced, intent—" Both men described this ravaging orchestra "like an insect swarm," with Langhorn adding, "that had to debilitate so they could conquer," a description Smith— by the way he frowned—found uncomfortable; Langhorn was being too lurid. But it was an event that called for luridness. As for the explosion or explosions, Smith said, "I didn't know where it came from; did they have *cannons*?" Whatever the source, the half face of the great monitor visage was halved again. As for the killing, Langhorn put it: "Random, like a lottery. And no one was resisting them." He said that to assert the barbarity of the invaders and also perhaps to accuse the slain of not confronting their murderers. He went on: "It was their way—for effect. To show us—to assert—expand—some evil energy."

Smith did not object to that purple prose. Both men were silent for a few seconds; then Smith spoke about Fukara's death. "I saw it from a distance. This shout—cry—from his ship; the body like some sack—of things—thrown over—I ran to him— That's when they attacked me...." After a pause: "I thought afterwards they took pleasure in it—but it wasn't pleasure. It was...." His eyes suddenly looked sharply back at us, with a bitter light of comprehension. "It was rage. They had a rage—madness—anger—at the world—made them crazy and hateful." His head bowed. Not looking at us he said, strangely, "Am I trying to be profound about this?"

It wasn't profound, but it was probably true. Abruptly Melissa said, "What were they wearing? How were they dressed?"

This seemed totally unimportant. Langhorn snapped, "You think with billowy shirts and three corner hats—peg legs?"

It suddenly struck me that Melissa wasn't having Blaise film this either. She had been caught up in the moment enough to forget to record it.

Langhorn: "They were dressed like men who work on a ship. I don't mean uniforms. Just clothes. T-shirts, shorts, jeans—whatever. The modern pirate."

Smith said, "It was the African who stopped them."

"The African." Of course, that was the generalization of Western whites, who might have reacted with amusement (and annoyance) over Africans describing an Italian or Scotsman as "the European." From the same continent, yes, but such different countries.

Smith was saying, "Strong looking, average height—odd face: like…almost a fish—bugged out eyes. But he certainly seemed in charge, shouting out commands in Chinese—"

"Dressed like the rest," said Langhorn curtly toward Melissa. For some reason he had been annoyed at her asking about the garb of the attackers. But now I had long observed that Melissa absorbed things visually.

Smith said, "I don't think he stopped them out of…mercy. Just that they had to get on to something else. They were taking too long with me—"

Rory: "An African leading Chinese pirates. Too bizarre." (You cannot *not* use that word through all this.)

Rita said, "Criminals are sometimes ecumenical. But you don't think of Asians and Africans."

Langhorn said, "He gave me the feeling he'd had some military background. You could see him in some African coup." Another western generalization.

"It was fast," said Smith. "That was the only saving grace. I was lying on the ground, bleeding, I don't think I was feeling the pain yet—before I knew it, the black ship and *The Gatherer* were going off." He pointed vaguely at some distance beyond the damaged plastic shelter.

Rory said, "Was it a worthwhile bounty for them?"

Langhorn frowned and shrugged. I thought any questions about "bounty" tasteless in this situation. Langhorn said, "Who knows? They've got another ship now. But was it a case of us just being there? It's as if they came here with purpose—"

Alluding to something he'd remarked before, Smith sighed and said, "It was Fukara." He let a pause fall, then: "Something with him and maybe there was more in his ship than the plastic for us." Abruptly he seemed to realize that that last word, "us," was subtly offensive. This surreal archipelago was *his* creation. "For me," he corrected.

I was thinking: crime, ravaging by pirates…a sort of conceptual performance art; yes, a statement of the moment that disappears—with time and the elements, like the sand drawings of certain religious disciplines: precisely planned, meticulously executed, then erased, effaced—gone.

Hurston said (he hadn't spoken for a while), "Do you have any idea what else there was on *The Gatherer?*"

Smith shrugged; and he winced at the movement. "He didn't tell me his business. He just…intimated—he had many activities."

I said, "Illegal?"

Smith winced again—at the question, or just more random pain? "He passes through so many countries—at least coasts; across the sea…. What's illegal somewhere isn't illegal…somewhere else."

Me again: "You know something and you're excusing him?"

Smith looked back at me with the face of someone for the moment past pain. "I said I didn't know all of his business. I didn't know *most* of it. But his type of entrepreneur…." His carefully probed his face with his hand, sighed once more. "But he's dead; we're forgetting—"

For a little while none of us said anything. Then Hurston said, "I've sent out a call. Someone should be along—eventually—"

"I'm all right, I'm all right," Smith insisted, not looking at any of us.

Hurston said, "I imagine your workers might want to leave. At least some of them."

Looking fully at Hurston, with sharply mustered strength Smith said, "We're staying." Then the strength seemed to leave, or at least need respite. He fell into silence again. His next words were less combative. "I'm staying, anyway. Anyone is free to go. Though I don't think many of them have homes—destinations."

21.

In a little while I left Gilligan's Island on a small boat with Melissa and Blaise to see up close the damage to the archipelago. I was beginning to think that the science article I was supposed to write would not be as meaningful as the larger thing—though who knew what that was—that seemed to continually beset the voyage of *The Argus* and Hurston's original intent.

"Once more *The Rocky Horror Picture Show*," said Blaise as he directed his camera at the ruins of the various islands.

The razed, giant computer monitor face was the most striking: horrific, grotesque—in some ways, I thought, like a sort of herald, the symbol of…something. In fact, this random ravaging was perhaps the touch needed to transform Smith's art into a message the artist could not have consciously intended, but which was the most true message of all.

I stepped out onto the small base from which the face rose. I found myself imagining all of these monitors in use, attached to computers, their screens once filled with a thousand things, from mundane recipes to research for school reports to pornography to the ten cheapest big cities in America. An emerging of myriad facts and images wrought into electronic actuality by disparate minds impelled by alternations of intent and boredom. And now—blank. More than blank: the artifacts that were, each one, nothing more than in a long line of the sequence of a product, now valueless, tossed aside, at the end of some odd journey in which the original purpose had been disposed of. I thought too that the daily things of our own lives eventually die their own inanimate deaths.

Though what we saw when we approached the ziggurat was more than a death, it was a desecration. There were Chinese symbols spray painted across the base on two sides. I suspected they were profane graffiti; I later found out I was right— something about the sexual acts of dogs being of the same nature as this faux plastic monument.

We pulled alongside this neo-Mayan creation, this 21st century art Alfredo had overseen that would—what had he said? Something about the levels of architecture. But memory, which could not allow everything to be sharp, would not be refreshed by the man himself. As we swung slowly around the ziggurat island we saw Alfredo's corpse, stretched out calmly on an uncompleted level. There was the instant denial—in each of us—that he was held in nothing worse than an exhausted sleep, the sleep of the recently violated, or at the worst the stupor of the wounded, but we each could see in another instant the aura of stiffness, of death. Blaise—without his camera; and Melissa did not protest—guided our boat to touch the island, got out, and went up to Alfredo, peered down at him, gently touched him. There was a pause as Blaise held himself like this, his hand withdrawn an inch from the body—as if he had suddenly been struck by something too astonishing to answer with movement. Then he straightened up and returned to us where we waited, on the rim of the island. "My God," he whispered hoarsely, "Why?" There was both fear and sorrow in his eyes. I couldn't exactly say what I felt. Melissa's face was blank; she appeared in a shock in which her own feelings were unnamable. This was a news story that had overcome her.

*　　　*　　　*

Back on Gilligan's Island Hurston was telling Langhorn and Smith the call he had sent out had been answered. "In a few hours…they should be here."

"They" turned out to be a ship on its own do-good mission, an NGO that brought surplus food from one part of the world to regions where surpluses were not common, from the haves to the have-nots, to climes of drought, famine and genocide. The vessel, *The Good Ship Bounty* (I would await Rita's first sarcasm about that) had been filling up along the wealthy ports of the Pacific rim, beginning with China, and was now headed to Sudan, "—and other parts of Africa," Hurston told us. I don't know if I was the first to say if not to think, "Why are they so far from the coast?—if they're going to—?"

Hurston looked at me as if I were questioning a very fortunate salvation: "Some storm—put them off course. You could call it the Hand of God—" Not that he said that with belief.

I don't think Smith was listening to any of this. I think the pain he was suffering and the violation he had suffered undermined his attentions.

*   *   *

The next few hours were odd, displaced—misplaced. We drifted about Gilligan's Island, had disjointed conversations with some of the workers, came back to Smith who, like a wounded animal (and he was) would not move from his lair. I heard him tell Langhorn, "It's plastic. It can be remolded." Yet the blackened areas I saw, the utter defacement: I didn't think "plastic surgery" would work in many cases.

Langhorn was saying, "I understand…you want it— completed."

Smith shot up—with no evidence of pain: "*Other* things I completed. I *complete*. This—it goes on. This—" he very unsmoothly gestured about him, wincing. "It's a setback."

22.

It was close to nightfall when *The Good Ship Bounty* came. Its affiliation was uncertain to me—and remained so. A Canadian and Australian official met with Hurston in the twilight and surveyed the damage, taking on board the injured—and the dead. Smith still refused to go. He was regarded as someone a little mad who would change his mind.

The officials also brought news: that somewhere to the southwest the pirate ship had been surrounded by the authorities of at least one Asian country. "Just one ship?" Hurston asked. A shrug was his reply.

In this mix of this international cooperation, I had the feeling the world had been coalesced into a jumble of people who would indeed work alongside each other, but perhaps all too much in the manner of Smith's archipelago, toiling in a goal that someone else had fixed, and moreover, not really understanding each other. And without understanding a true community could not grow.

While Hurston continued to ask the men questions about the pirates, and in particular "the African—they said he was in charge." The Canadian, who actually looked like an Englishman out of the time of the-sun-never-sets-on the Empire, tall, ramrod straight, tight moustache—but who spoke with an accent that recalled to me the American Midwest—related a surreal story about a Somali (well, of course) who had "succeeded—if you can call it that—at various criminal activities, but finally could not work with the Muslim fanatics there, decided on his own 'enterprise'...." The official went on: "The Somali—his name isn't known, he's just called

something that's translated as 'Wrath'—somehow *franchised*"
(the Canadian smiled; it was so American a word) "the
operation the Somalis do so well now—piracy—to some
Asians. They've taken probably a dozen ships by now; I think
every one they sold back for ransom. They haven't *specifically*
made the news, though…."

They would now; Melissa had Blaise back at it. He was
filming away. The Canadian made a few glances and smiles at
the camera. The Australian was for the most part silent, not at
all the stereotype of the garrulous Aussie; he granted Blaise
one brief glance and one forced smile—while the Canadian
was adding, "I think they've got him—them—now, though. I
don't think pirates can really escape today."

*   *   *

I'll shoot a little ahead in time. What we found out a few
days later was that the pirate ship had indeed been captured,
and the activities of the aforenamed Wrath and his crew ended.
Though the story, filtered through several avenues, was not cut
and dry. There had been a battle. The pirates declared they held
a hostage from the archipelago; but it had been a ruse. That had
gained them some time, but in all human things time runs out.
But time had allowed the pirates further movement, with the
"authorities" following—right into the center of the Great
Pacific Garbage Patch. When the pursuers learned that
everyone from the plastic islands had been accounted for, they
closed in on the pirates, preparing to do battle.

So: in the center of the Patch—and abruptly trapped, at least
bogged down in the glimmering.

Yes, the glimmering. From the accounts we heard it was
nothing less. I'm sure it disconcerted (at the very least) both
the pursued and pursuers. The latter neared the former in this
odd transformation of humanity's plastic. It was a bright day,

as I read in the account of one of the "authorities." I'm sure it was roughly translated, but it said to the effect that the pirates—some of them, anyway—saw the glimmering as supernatural. "There were such cries from their ship…. Some thought we had done it, created this. A technology to trap them. Technology or superstition. One of them jumped from the ship into the water. Fear sometimes draws people to the thing of fear itself. This man drowned. We could not go after him. The pirates were shooting at us. Not very well, but they continued. You could sense their weapons were helpless, but still dangerous, of course.

"The black man, the African, was on deck. He made angry gestures to us. A fist he waved. It took us too long to come right alongside the ship. There was battle. The African, two of the Chinese tried to escape in a lifeboat. We caught them— caught the boat. The black man jumped, swam in that shining water. He wasn't swimming well. He was darkness in that unnatural light. Even some of us felt a little superstitious. But we caught him. Had to shoot him in the arm—"

I didn't know if the glimmering drifted off and the authorities and the commandeered pirate ship made their way back free of the strange jelly plastic, or if they had to go inch by inch, through the morass.

I said to Langhorn: "But wait. Where's *The Gatherer*? They took it—"

He shrugged. "That's the mystery. Gone. Though I heard it through someone who heard it through someone that one of the pirates alleged the glimmering—though he used a different word for it—said *The Gatherer* had already been captured by the glimmering, gone under. The authorities say they don't believe it's possible."

That image: of an entire ship, sucked down, into the

glimmering. Could that really be possible?

I found the story of the pirates incomplete. I did not know for some time the full extent of what had happened to Wrath and his crew. I doubted I'd see this on the cable news channels. Perhaps, I thought, after Melissa's documentary is shown, we would find out.

23.

The Argus went on to Asia. Hurston spent the rest of the voyage going over the data with Rita—and, I think, becoming a bit closer to her—at least socially. But that's speculation. Perhaps he remained faithful to that fiancé on shore.

We docked at Hong Kong. In this striking cosmopolitan city of the East (to which we arrived at by going west—it's all relative), I found myself walking through its crowded streets, looking at huge signs, neon advertisements, the lettering of shops with their foreign symbols, thinking that someone from another planet would be hard put to recognize the written language of any earthly culture unless it were in a context that pointed towards its function. And thinking, because of the middle passage I'd been through on *The Argus*, of the innumerable computers, the countless PCs and laptops, printers, cell phones, etc. that were raised above the streets in tier after tier of offices and apartments, every wondrous device destined by the gravity of time and use to an end that could possibly be one of wise recycling (more and more countries were enacting laws), but more likely to wind up rimming a town like Guiya, which I visited with Hurston and the rest of the crew, a wretched place in Guangdong Province, inland from Hong Kong. This was the area the English used to refer to as Canton. It was a drive of many hours on a hot day of smeared clouds to behold hill after hill of e-trash, like the geography of a post-apocalypse robot world, heaps and heaps of our castoff technology, electronics and plastics, shattered monitors and snakes of twisted wires, without the art of an Arturo Smith to make them interesting. And parts of everyday electronic products had been dumped in the river—half sticking out of the water like corpses long ago murdered, but whose infective decay still flowed down stream.

Hurston said, "Even before this century, by the end of the '90s, this place had become the biggest waste site of e-trash in China."

There were indoor workshops, most of which I could not enter for very long. How could anyone breathe that air for an hour, for hours, days, weeks—months—years? Whether faces looked back at me from clear air that was nonetheless contaminated, or a hazy atmosphere clearly polluted, I could read no "explanation" for the suffering (is that the word?) here.

I guess poverty was—is—the explanation.

The open air workshops were foul enough themselves—with the added horror of the sense that these pollutants were escaping immediately into the air and land and water. Like archaeologists in a hell (what had that young woman of the Gulf of Mexico's coast said to me?) workers pick through, dismantle, take apart circuit boards, printers, old TV tubes. And like that video from Africa, a woman and child sit by a fire that melts the plastic from wires, the horrible smoke curling about them like the acrid wind of the damned. The boy coughs, the woman blinks her reddened eyes. The official who grants us this tour is stern-eyed and gives voice to no lament or even sympathy. Then again, he only knows a few words of English. But his eyes say volumes to me. Hurston had used some connection, some international environmental connection, to gain us this tour of the inferno; it is useful to have lived a lifetime of being rich and then turning that money into good works. The official did say something clipped and abrupt, and Hurston turned to us and said—and paraphrased—flatly, "Without this these people would have no work."

At that unfeeling remark, the expression on Melissa's face was one I had not seen before. (Though I think I've said that about her a few times.) Hurston's pull had not extended to allowing Melissa—that is, Blaise—to film the apocalyptic factory. Perhaps Melissa's expression was simply the culmination of frustration and annoyance at being stayed from the exercise of her profession. But there seemed more. She did take notes. And was frowned at for doing so by the official, but he gave no cry to stop. And he must have seen Blaise sketching on a small pad a few ugly scenes. I hadn't known before that Blaise's talent for the visual extended to drawing. At any rate, the official had to know we all looked on this with horror. Though he had the moral trump of knowing—and knowing *we* knew—that most of this e-trash had come from the United States. I literally stepped on a rectangular plate affixed to the side of a dismembered monitor that read "Property Environmental Protection Agency, Washington, D.C."

I thought of the bits and bytes, the megabytes and gigabytes of information this trash had held. Or still did. Many businesses—especially the government—and many individuals have the data effaced from their computers before trashing them, but whether that data had died in some antiseptic "defacing" program or service, or had died here, among the hell-damned workers and plastic fires, I had the sense that this trash was indeed the parts of a corpse that had once held a life of sorts: our time's redundant God of Information, the incessant increase of which has led to this incessant cannibalized graveyard of technology, which we, its creators in a very real way, had to acknowledge with horror. Like Yahweh horrified at the use to which his Tree of Life— Knowledge—Good and Evil—had come?

"One hundred thousand people do this work," said the official. "Many, many come here to work."

My thoughts went on: a slew of souls fallen to the abuse of technology's angel.

"What did people do here—before?" asked Hurston.

The official considered, searching his English. "Farming." He frowned. "There is still some farming—sold outside— here."

"Outside," repeated Hurston. "Do the farmers here eat their own crops?"

The official frowned again and did not answer. He led us on.

We passed a giant hill of e-trash upon which workers clambered up and clambered down, clutching electronic parts, faces dirty and sweat stained: Lilliputians damned in a circle of hell of which Dante had not conceived.

I watched Jorges watching all this quietly. He had been very inward since the death of Emile. Trying to be casual, I said to him, "What do you think of all this?"

He looked at me with eyes that would not admit what he thought. "Terrible for these people."

I wondered, but did not say, if he thought this might have been his lot had he been born Chinese. And caught myself. That was arrogant. What if *I* had been born into this poverty here?

He read my thoughts—perhaps it wasn't hard. "You think…I can be like them."

I tried to cover myself artfully. "Any of us could be."

"No, you don't think it that." I was a little startled. It was the first time I'd seen Jorges be confrontational. "You haven't been close to—to that." He gestured to a skinny, weathered man—who was thirty, looking fifty?—with a tattered basket that brimmed with circuit boards. The man's forearms and hands were dirty and bleeding.

So I said it gently. "You've been close to that?"

He nodded. "Why I came to America."

I gave my own nod. After a pause I said, "But do you think differently—seeing this—about this…crossing the ocean was supposed to—?" I was faltering for words.

Jorges said, simply, "I see everywhere, trash. You have people, you have garbage."

I wanted to continue this, but an unusual scene distracted me—distracted all of us. Or rather, a person who made the scene about us even more unusual.

In the near distance, out of a thick swirl of acrid grey smoke that seemed almost woven, a woman appeared, an old-looking middleaged woman stepping from between two half obscured hillocks of e-trash. She wore a coil of copper about her head, and a dress—if you could call it that—of circuit boards banging against her body. She had some fabric underneath, but most of her was covered by some artifact of technological trash. The earrings that dangled on either side of her face were thin golden wires from which a letter key from a computer keyboard were attached. On her wrists were bracelets of wires, the plastic partly burned away, giving an intentional or unintentional effect of color and dullness, hardness and softness.

The woman was gesturing and calling out to the workers, who responded with something that was more than friendliness, though something I couldn't quite describe.

The official made a groaning sound. It was the recognition of—and resignation to—a familiar unpleasantness. Hurston caught that note of habitual tension and asked, "Who's that?"

"Crazy woman. Year ago she start. Some call her—" He

shook his head at a great folly. "Some call her Kaun Yin." He barked a short laugh.

I said, "What does that mean?"

"Great Mother of China."

The woman, leaving of a veil of smoke behind, moved through smaller wraiths of smoke, approached and passed through huddled knots of workers, talking to them, touching them in a definitely ethereal manner, as if she visited this hell from a better place. At least a place understanding of their woe. The copper on her hair and the duller metals of the circuit boards caught whatever sun made its way through the polluted atmosphere.

Despite himself, the official told us more, his manner agitated but helpless. (Then again, perhaps he too was drawn in.) Kaun Yin was the name of an ancient Chinese goddess, and this latest incarnation, this crazy woman from the e-trash heaps that had been generated by 20th and 21st century science, bore to these wretched hordes bound to burning wires and tearing apart mother boards, the presence of a promise. The legend of Kaun Yin is that she will live on Earth until every human being is freed from pain.

Jorges watched her intently. Blaise was drawing her. On the whiteness of his pad a figure was outlined that looked like it wore the armor of medieval Asia. Well, this woman was of the past—and she was of the future. Melissa was muttering, clearly frustrated she could not have *this* as one of her many preserved images that had assaulted us since we'd left San Francisco. Rory had a look I could not read at all, and Rita—well, she began to walk toward the woman. Hurston and the official called out after Rita; but it was inevitable.

The woman noted the approach of the foreigner through the debris and swirls of smoke, this beautiful woman from the other side of the Earth, well fed and proportioned much more like a goddess than the pseudo-Kaun Yin, who faced the slow advance of Rita with a curious and wary look. The workers too, of course, looked at Rita with a wariness—and other emotions just as universal.

Rita stopped before her and said, loudly: "You're wonderful."

The woman spread her arms; technological artifacts dangled and jangled. She declared something solemn. Rita called back to the official. "What'd she say?"

He shrugged, called back, "I can't hear."

Rita looked annoyed, then changed her expression and reached out to touch one of the circuit boards that slapped against the woman's torso. Kaun Yin smiled. Did she take that as an act of worship? Her nostrils dilated. In response, I coughed. To take in more of that air—

Rita broke into a wide smile and a soft laugh. Now I understood what her "wonderful" had meant: most absurd. I felt sorry for the mad woman who had taken the artifacts of her oppression and had tried to convert them into something beyond this ugly toil. A shred of foul smoke passed across Kaun Yin's face as she tried to smile back at Rita—but she was sensing something she did not like or at least was not comfortable in embracing. Perhaps this e-trash goddess wondered if she could draw this stranger into her realm—or if the stranger was too potent a disruption. Her arm went up, bent at the elbow, palm facing inward, her face looking at the palm, as if in soliloquy with herself, or reading some palmistry that foretold something as imminent as the present. Then abruptly she turned from Rita and strode back into the midst of her people. But she did dart one half glance back at this gorgeous American-British woman, made some enigmatic gesture, and called out a word or words that made Rita once again demand of the official: "What? What?"

This time he had heard. He translated: "You came here; go." A statement, and a wish. I watched Kaun Yin move off into the smoke and topography of e-trash, the faces of her people looking at her not so much with hope as a sort of recognition.

The official was saying to us, "She is crazy, but maybe good—for them."

"For them." He, of course, was not among "them." Though perhaps Jorges should have asked this bureaucratic, unsympathetic man what if *he* had been born into this realm in which the most profitable work proffered was gleaning the marketable fragments and shards from the electronic trash of the West—and, increasingly, the East, too? The poor workers who had to not only bear the garbage of the foreigner but of their own country. *There* was the grimmest heart of this despair: betrayal. It took from these Chinese the "out" of pointing elsewhere. Their oppressors were their mirrored selves.

The image of the bizarre woman persisted in my mind. She was a creation of her environment, as we all are. Whether the environment is a hodgepodge, a trash heap of our creation, a haphazard—and hazardous—milieu, whose surreal strains work accidents of mythological passion, or the controlled avenues of a city, the well ordered décor of a home, we were, we are shaped in a way never quite anticipated.

I thought of following her to whatever hovel she lived in, forcing the official or someone else to translate, to hear the pith and outline of her story, to set what would surely be crazy words and perspective against her crazy world, to show my reader how it fit, how the latter demanded the former, how mad environs created mad gods and goddesses the wretched might touch, might imagine as not only a protection but a catalyst for some healing apocalypse—I wanted to speak with her not to portray her madness as delusion but with a sympathy, empathy—

Yet I did not follow her disappearance into that foul haze. Enough madness had come to me in the midst of this journey of *The Argus*; perhaps I was just too tired to seek more. I looked to the rest of my crew members; Jorges eyed me as if he intuited and even shared my thoughts—and knew, as I suddenly knew, it was wiser to let all this alone.

*   *   *

In a hotel that rose above the great teeming city of Hong Kong I looked from this aerie on the masses flowing through their metropolis and became struck by—and sucked into?—an almost transcendent reverie. It was not unlike when I sometimes watched the sea move by the ship. But the peace and reach of my psyche was abruptly broken by the phone, which at first seemed a sound from neither my inner world nor the world outside, that spread out below. It was a call from an editor for an assignment that would draw me away from the crew of *The Argus*, and yet it was inextricably linked to the journey and mission we'd all undertaken. A journey which by now I realized probably had no culmination but was one of continuous stops or stages: an odyssey none of us had chosen, or certainly had anticipated.

24.

I would not be interviewing the pirate Wrath for any popular science magazine; my being part of the crew of *The Argus* (and the fact that I could write, of course) gave me enough credentials to land the assignment for *Vanity Fair*, and what would be the most I'd ever been paid for an article.

There were stipulations by the UN authorities who held Wrath: I was not allowed to specifically name the location of his detention. I wasn't sure if that bespoke of something ominous in the nature of the powers-that-be, or indicated a deserved caution.

Wrath had agreed to see me; that hadn't been a surprise. In our time—for a long time now—everyone, saint, politician, criminal, athlete, scientist, whatever, we all live in a realm of instant publicity, the mirror of global news, whether of events major or minor that appeared to make more substantial our deeds. Wrath, if certainly not a household name, might become one—or, at least an interesting item on the evening news. I could see Melissa eagerly, luridly captioning his story. And then there might be a twenty minute news magazine piece….

And the issue wasn't whether Wrath sought a "wider" recognition or not. Long before this time, it has been the habit of criminals to give interviews. Each of us believes our own stories, in our words, told with sincere expression, will gain sympathy—or, even, approval.

Not that individuals like Wrath saw themselves as criminals. I assumed that slant to his tale before meeting him. I guessed he would see himself more as a Third World entrepreneur, though I was sure he would not use that description. He was the beset rebel fighting the ugly circumstances of the life in which chance had placed him.

And me, the African-American, interviewing the African pirate—this was a connection that hung in my psyche in more than subtle ways. In fact, after having gotten the assignment, a sort of flickering light bulb went through my mind: *Oh, so maybe that's why they want me to write it….*

*   *   *

I was escorted into a featureless room by a slim Asian who

wore navy blue pants, a white short sleeved shirt and the sort of black-billed, white topped hat, like the captain of a cruise ship might wear. I say "Asian" because I'm not very good at determining if someone is Chinese, Japanese, Korean, Vietnamese, etc. No, I'm not saying they all look alike (like they used to say about black people); I can discern the individual, just not always the ethnicity. Anyway, in a very formal accent he told me to wait a few minutes—but Wrath was brought in sooner than that, by two burly men with berets and camouflage gear, as if they'd just ferreted him out in the bush. By turns seemingly wary and indifferent, they would linger behind Wrath throughout our interview, at what you might call a respectful distance, giving a deception of privacy. One of the guards was plainly African (and yes, Africa has its different peoples, too), the other European—very fair; Scandinavian, it seemed. Asian, African, European—a too studied attempt at diversity?

The room had two very small slits for windows: rectangles a few inches wide and about a foot or so long: as if in pitiful recognition that there should be some light in this official space. I caught, just barely, the wave of a green frond in bright hot light. Again, I was not allowed to say exactly where this room was, but I don't think I'd be violating any agreement to say it was in a warm climate.

Wrath awaited me at a table, dark body tight with a peculiar tension. He wore a clean—obviously new—dark olive short sleeved shirt and pants. There was a band of white gauze around one sinewy forearm; I recalled he'd been shot. I could not exactly describe the expression with which he greeted me. He was waiting for my reactions to him for him to react to me.

Wrath was young; I'd say 25. Though he had already had a full career. From working the African e-trash heaps as a boy to a Somali-sponsored pirate as a teenager, he had graduated to his own command, his own crew; and then, like a baseball player signed on with a team that could bring him larger rewards, a larger scope, an Asian underworld concern, apparently believing it could effect piracy more efficiently, offered Wrath a wider sphere of business. True 21st century globalism. At any rate, it seemed he had been "successful."

Though I would find there was more to his story.

He was young but homely. He had large eyes that bugged out of his head, a characteristic of those with a thyroid condition. His face too seemed pushed forward, his lips with certain expressions jutting out, like a fish. But he was muscular. His strong looking body and odd-looking face gave him the overall appearance of a gargoyle. I soon realized the mind in that body was sharp. The boy who had been burning and peeling plastic from wires and then had become the young man who could command the pirate ship of an Asian cartel had to possess a reservoir of intelligence, no matter how misdirected. That's my assessment—*our* assessment: misdirection. He had been presented with a certain life: he had survived as he could. The purist might argue that even the boy melting computer wires was aware there was another world beside piracy. As we are aware that some people are born heirs and heiresses to fortunes. Wrath's rise to piracy was fantasy enough, just a closer fantasy, one barely possible—and so he had made it possible.

I saw the intelligence, at least the skill to do what was necessary, from our first words. I thanked him, like any polite journalist habitually does, for agreeing to talk to me—though thinking about what he and his crew had done on the plastic islands, I phrased it: "I'm glad you could talk to me."

He said, "I can't talk all your words, but I tell you truth."

Was the substance of his statement wisdom or the chance of his limited English? He would "tell" me "truth." Maybe every deep conversation is like this—maybe every journalistic interview: the one questioned has to translate the inner truth the other apprehends in the self—while something always gets lost in the translation.

If Wrath's English was limited, the limit contained a large enough facility of communication. In fact, his facility with languages was practically unlimited. He could get by in French, English, Arabic, Japanese, Chinese and several African dialects: Djerma, Lingala, Yoruba, Bantu and more. If this young man had not grown up in such abject poverty, been orphaned as a child, been thrown into working the e-trash heaps of Africa at some uncounted age, what would he have become?

That's what I led him to speak of first—or did he lead me? "Parents die AIDS." Was this embellishment or true? "Live with uncle, give him money make, keep some. Keep more." He was already working in the e-trash heaps. "But—" He spread out his hands, indicating whatever "money make," whatever "more," it could not fill his grasp, it could not fill what was necessary for life.

Though he was good enough to make a little more than the others. In the flames that melted the wires he could "stop breathe long"; he could "run out, run in," bring out of his harsh extraction more than his wretched peers.

Peers. Did he see these others? See himself, in them? Redundant selves, struggling in the mirror? I asked, "Were you angry you had to do this?"

"Now angry. Not angry ago. Just want to breathe. See without eyes hurt."

But perhaps that is our lives here: seeing involves some sort of hurt.

He related to me—as if a fact of distant memory that had little to do with him now—that after the death of his parents (close upon each other it seemed; from his scant words I saw a man and woman in near order expiring in some poor hut, on a sick bed of dirty sheets) he had been raised—or rather passed along to—relatives and then eventually partial strangers, then complete strangers who possessed little altruism but were more inclined to regard the orphan as a means of profit. So the orphan had been dissolved into the lowest common denominator of existence: a virtual child slave working (and living) at one of the e-trash operations in eastern Congo.

"That's your country, the Congo?" The look that answered, both blank and scolding, made me intuit what he explained. He was not sure just what country in which he had been born— and seemed indifferent to that lack to which most of us would feel as a void. His more mature, at least coherent memories had been at that work in the Congo, where, among all the unending bounty to be extracted from techno trash (the century's transubstantiation), he drew from electronic debris the tantalum made from coltan ore that was in fact being mined close by, near the Rwandan border.

I tried to go back. "Do you remember your parents saying where they were from?" He shook his head slightly, as if too much motion might dislodge too much memory. Then he said he could not even be sure his parents had died from AIDS; that was simply what he recalled being told. Clearer were the memories—if they were also chaotic and repetitive—of being moved to different e-trash sites, and then eventually being taken as "a good worker" by some "company big man": an African, being moved to more sites (it was an enterprise without borders), where his menial skill was further worked— and, also, his not so menial skills. "I speak all things," he said, a child slave laborer with the boon and curse of Babel on his tongue. This was now being noticed, at least a little. Though to this day Wrath could hardly read—mostly labels, from the goods he worked at; an outcome of circumstance, not ability. He had lived in the world of face-to-face interaction. His survival and safety meant the voice, understanding the spoken words—and schemes—of others.

I asked him about the "schemes" of the "big company man." All I got was that he was tall, had a shaved head and talked little. Had he understood the orphan's polyglot brilliance? But what reason could he have had to talk much to his slaves, who endured a physically polluted life, a spiritually polluted life in wresting from technological trash anything that was worth anything? Ultimately the man remained a shadow in Wrath's memory, only a little more palpable than his parents had been.

That wraith passed from Wrath's life and a more definite form entered, who sought something worth a great deal from e-trash. With a nod that was gesture and some barked word that was like an abrupt signature on a contract, Wrath had been sold to a new e-trash entrepreneur: none other than Fukara, the man Wrath or at least his crew would murder. And in an instant I knew the Asian had established a history with the child slave prodigy that had led to this specific violence. Like some 19th European colonists, Fukara had descended upon Africa with a vision of material gain and blatant exploitation. Wrath said Fukara had had a vast e-trash operation in—well, several countries. Wrath seemed as hesitant about borders and nations as if he were a diplomat confessing an indifference to the nature of any principality he might serve.

But I was still swept in the surprise of Fukara.

In one way, the new owner of the child Wrath (older now, but still child) put him at the same tasks to which he had been bound—but with an end more focused. Fukara wanted the gold in computers. More and more I had been doing my research, discovering the somber facts of the trash of our technology, discovering that the small amount of gold in the electronics of our Information Age could be made large by the ubiquity of its use. If one could extract all the traces of gold from every discarded computer, it would equal the great mining ventures of any time in history. A metric ton of circuit boards can yield anywhere from 40-800 times the gold from gold ore regularly mined in the U.S. By the turn of the 20th century into the 21st, 200 metric tons of gold had been used in electronics.

Fukara had no vision to extract all this waiting gold other than to subsume it with thousands of workers: something like the overwhelming invasion of an insect colony. As Wrath talked on I had the vision of some giant gold edifice being swarmed over by Lilliputian scavengers—a vision I was apparently lost in for more than a moment as I found Wrath looking at me warily. I nodded, to show that I was listening again.

He gave me wary looks often. Or looks that might have been other than wary: surprise and cautious that he and I were of the same heritage. Once I caught him tilting his head, as if his eyes needed to receive me from another perspective, to test if any original assessment were true or not.

If Fukara focused on his vision of extracting gold from electronics, he did come to recognize the qualities of young Wrath, who by now not only had so much experience in the treasures of e-trash, but could be a translator for the workers that had been gathered from a number of countries; he could ride over the babble, smooth confusions. So by the age of sixteen Wrath was de facto supervisor to not only his peers but younger children—and even those older than himself, whose natural resentment at being directed by such youth was stayed by Fukara, who could be harsh enough to ensure compliance to the task in which he had gathered so many.

"Was he violent?" I asked. Wrath shook his head. It was something lingering outside the realm of illustration. Though that struck me first as an evasion, if an involuntary one. "A Japanese, an Asian…over Africans? How could he—?" I looked for the words: "Hold that?" Wrath widened his eyes a little, as if this increased view of the whites around his irises could force some sight—insight—into me.

I had my own insight, or profound-seeming "explanation." Perhaps in a wholly unconscious way the African of the 21st century, heir to lost kingdoms, slave raiders and colonial depredations could no longer be roused against the race of the oppressor as in the not so old days. There had been centuries of oppression by Europeans—and Arabs, too, who were in the slave trade longer than the Europeans; and then, through most of the 20th century, that rising wave of revolt, of returning to the continent's own native chaos as opposed to the structured prison of the foreign. Now, after all these centuries, and the struggles of revolution, which had brought the facades of democracy, the surrealities of egomaniacal dictators, the African of the new millennium had been worn into the revelation that evil and oppression came in any color (after all, Africans had sold Africans to the foreign slavers) and could be no more affronted about a Japanese controlling their lives in the e-trash heaps as they would be at the shadowy black that had been Wrath's earlier "owner."

This was perhaps a rise of enlightenment that was not quite enlightenment, more like surrender, a recognition of a common, debased humanity with little hope for the future, and as Wrath stared at me as these thoughts grew within and shot through me, I knew he would reject me if I spoke them; they would fall against the stare of his protruding eyes, as some esoteric incoherence that could only be regarded as apart from his life's rough passage. Before the stare I unconsciously gave in turn, those eyes blinked, as the polyglot mouth did tell me—in contradiction to that earlier shrug—about Fukara's violence. Though it was a mental, emotional violence, hardly a physical one. Wrath used the word "cruel": exactly what he said was, "Cruel to heart," and tapped his chest awkwardly, with handcuffed fists. I understood that Wrath had needed a few minutes to translate to himself what could be meant by violence—even if I had been thinking of physical violence alone. The spirit has its will within the weak flesh, but the will is often as delicate as it is strong.

Fukara tortured his workers with some capitalist techniques. He called for certain quotas. He first set these as rewards; those attaining them would get extra money. I asked, "Were most of the workers living where you were doing this? Was it a compound, where you had to spend it right there?"

Wrath nodded. His expression gave no dismay at this abuse of capitalism.

Fukara penalized workers who fell too far behind their quota. Not so much as to provoke revolt, but to urge that extra effort, so that each wretched worker had the incentive (poor use of the word) so as to not fall further into wretchedness.

I said, "Quotas—how? Pieces, weight—?"

"Each different," said Wrath.

The gold was weighed, other items were counted by the piece. Fukara was focused on the gold, but he did not disdain the value of other metals. Drop by metallic drop the gold was extracted by the many workers. "How many?" I asked Wrath, who was poor with numbers beyond basic amounts; he spread out his hands, stretched long scarred fingers, burned and scraped too many times in the e-trash fires and debris; he indicated many, many times ten.

If Wrath could not ascertain a rough estimate of this slave labor force, or the gold he and others extracted, he did realize he was one of the better workers, and so had a possibility at the prize Fukara next offered: living quarters that were a step above the squalid huts the workers lived in—a small cabin "on little hill—flowers." My God, a house on a hill with flowers— and: "Water." Water! Probably polluted with whatever leached from the fevered work at the e-trash heap, but still manna to the slaving masses. Water unlimited, while to the sweating masses it was rationed. I thought of being perpetually parched—and stinking.

"I want house," said Wrath.

He got it. Earnest and capable—or desperate and longing— Wrath achieved the house in which he had four quiet, clean walls to himself, flowers in front (an especially ironic addition, I thought), and the elevation of the little hill, so he seemed, at the end of the grueling day, apart—and above—from his peers: successful.

It was a slice of heaven for him, something unattainable that he had attained. Fukara had smiled upon him.

I asked, "Was he there all the time?" Wrath shook his head. "Well, I'm sure he didn't live there," I added.

Where did the entrepreneurial Japanese live? In some quarters certainly more comfortable than Wrath's newly gained sanctuary. Or perhaps he did in fact rough it. Wrath indicated Fukara travelled about to other operations.

"Did he give someone in each of those places a prize house?"

Wrath looked at me in apparent surprise. It seems he hadn't

thought of that. Well, misery and striving in that misery makes one focus on the immediate. And of course there would be a problem with the "prize house." Wrath pointed at me with a forefinger. "Only month. Must do good—better—still—to keep—" He strung those words out, like a man speaking through the pain of a wound. If the keeper of the house didn't do "better," the next super-worker would get the house. Wrath commented that he did not know this at first. It had been in the fine print of Fukara's vocal offers. Or perhaps Fukara hadn't said anything like that at all, but came to the obvious use of further incentive after he had congratulated Wrath on gaining the house.

It wasn't that Wrath slacked off. "I do hard," he said. But that small degree of comfort he had grasped because of straining past the others had made him a little less desperate enough (even with the threat of loss before him) so that another worker, more than twice his age, someone the teenager could see only as old, gained the house through his own toilsome plunder of techno debris; and so, after those very few weeks, Wrath, with the abrupt taste of something better, was returned to his former station.

What bitterness, what railing at the gods must have at least turmoiled within Wrath—especially as Fukara still treated Wrath as his golden polyglot boy, with the same responsibilities and no lessened desire for gold. "He smile, he work me, he tell me plans—future—" But Wrath's only future, as he saw it, was to get back into the house.

What a devious circumstance had been thrust upon Wrath; instead of thinking of escaping from this life, he thought of attaining the circumstance's pitiful reward.

Which he did attain once more. As he had lost the house, he won it back—barely. He and the man who had unseated him

("Thin, bone, big head—"; you had the impression of a cadaver)—the prodigy and the thin man having their gold weighed daily, the ledger of their extractions of everything imaginable to be extracted, the contest day after day creating the larger contest, and, "By this much," Wrath said, putting thumb and forefinger parallel and hardly separated in front of my face, Wrath returned to the house. Fukara had cheered and clapped at the return of his prodigal.

"But not same," Wrath frowned, and lids closed over bugged out eyes in the memory of it. When he had first achieved the house he felt he had gained it once and for all, that it had been at the end of the struggles of years, a large reward for him, a deserved reward. But: "Feel him still there," spat out Wrath, the presence of the man just departed not so much a lingering aftermath but a herald for what could happen in another month. Wrath could lose the house again, struggle, get it back, lose it—or only gain it once in a while—or not at all, ever again. He looked from the windows, out over the flowers, to the e-trash heaps, the workers bound to the shift that had followed him (often work went on through the night, the hell of the heaps lighted garishly, the spirit of the workers kept from the beneficence of day) and realized (if he didn't necessarily have the word for it) that the house was a distraction, a *deception*, for those to whom the one creating the deception thought of as little more than slaves—as nothing.

For Wrath it was like a lover returning to an unfaithful partner—but the infidelity here was large, very large, larger than even Fukara, who continued to applaud the boy's continued good work…though work that did not gain him the house again; and when another occupant took it, Wrath said to himself he would never accept the house again, ever; and he looked on Fukara with deepening hatred. The man he had seen as an exotic possibility to something beyond this life was nothing more than the constant betrayer.

If only Fukara had cultivated Wrath more logically, used him, schooled him, let him keep that sustenance of shelter, like an older exec mentoring a younger for the good of them both, for the good of the company. But that was an ideal that could not exist here.

The sense and sensing of betrayal that had grown large in Wrath would be agitated into explosion by a final incident. Of course, the most "final incident" was Fukara's murder; but this was a prior clash that drove such an anger—and a perspective—into Wrath that his time with Fukara had to end:

A skinny, overworked girl who had suffered as Wrath had suffered, who appeared at the e-trash heap after Wrath had lost the house for the second time. His anger and his disillusionment could only fuel his ardor—had it even become love?—for the female version of himself: a girl who bore through the wretchedness, extracted profits from trash, and who was pleased that Wrath knew her tongue—Bantu. They cleaved together, cleaved hearts and flesh by the crevices and privacies of the trash heaps, a lovemaking that had to be uncomfortable among the techno debris, with Wrath often thinking that if only he had been able to keep the house with the flowers, both of them could have lived there....

It was an intuition of hearts. The girl had had a path Wrath could well understand. Her mother had died of malaria, her father had been executed because of his association with a group that aimed to overthrow the government. The last time she had seen her mother had been on her deathbed, the face looking up and seeing what the living here can't see; the last time the girl had seen her father was in a courtroom ("More guard than people," Wrath said she said, indicating sentinels of authority weren't people, and with a glance at the two guards who stood dumbly, indicating their status was similar)—in a courtroom where the father stood before a judge who boomed out the charges while the father looked ahead, also seeing something those not in his situation could not see. And so the girl lived through a passage of relatives, was eventually urged—or even sold—into the e-trash life, a slim, small girl, "Almost child," said Wrath, "but *eyes*—" and left off on that emphasis, intimating the girl had *seen*, seen too much to be a girl now, seen the seeing-ness of her mother and father, and then come to the rough, toxic toil of her hands.

There was a pause, a long pause as Wrath looked downward, or somewhere past both me and himself, into his own private seeing, that private place of memory and comprehension that is just as unknowable to another as the last seeing of the dying and the captured seeing of the condemned, and when he spoke again, he did try (out of obligation? defiance?—or just the vanity of storytelling?) to describe in some way the brief time of his love: "Rest. Rest with her. She talk. I listen. Better— better than sleep." (I noted Wrath used "than" more than once in telling his story to me, grasping all the implications of the foreign word of both visceral and abstract comparison.) I wondered: had Wrath, in all the days of his labor, "hurt"? Had there been rage and pain at the ugliness and bondage of it, and hence the rage, the wrath of Wrath? Or had he only known the "hurt" when it had ceased in the presence of the girl? Like a pain one is so acclimated to that one forgets its presence, only realizing that presence in its sporadic absence. At any rate, Wrath's few words told me a full story, and perhaps a more truthful one than a story thick with protestation and lament.

If their meetings were in whatever privacies they could find, their togetherness was known. But whether it had been secret or open, Fukara probably would have done the same. One day the girl was working by Wrath; Fukara came and took her away. "He just say: 'Here,'" Wrath mumbled, with the menace of past anger. It might have been a casual summons from an overseer to a worker, but each of them knew otherwise. Wrath and the girl looked at each other. Fukara repeated his order, more sternly.

"I say: 'With me!'" Wrath pounded his chest before me, the handcuffs that hit his flesh sign that he would always be bound.

The guards, our guards here, gave us a wary look.

Wrath gave no further detail other than that he attacked Fukara. It was the unforgivable sin for a slave. He was subdued—not gently—by the ubiquitous guards—or supervisors—whatever the word; the girl, first complaining, then mutely, went off with Fukara. Perhaps she understood this would be the better circumstance—under the circumstances she was in. Though surely it would be like Wrath's house: gained, lost, maybe gained again—maybe.

"I stay ground. No work, no work." That was what he had yelled. What would have happened if one of Fukara's associates—a Chinese man; there were always foreigners around Fukara—had not just then offered to buy Wrath? Dazed, beaten, the house on the hill, the girl—events of mockery in his life, Wrath watched Fukara go from cursing him to praising Wrath's skills. "Man say he know, he know," said Wrath, which meant to me that the Chinese had noted Wrath's qualities before and saw this sexual blowup as the perfect opportunity to get some desirable—profitable—bit of human merchandise at a good price.

In short order Wrath was leaving with the Chinese man— and more than half willingly. And so the echoes of Africa's past and slavery was again echoed in the 21st century, the beginning of the third millennium of the Christians, a slavery once chosen that had become no other choice. Well, suicide— Wrath had seen that: three he said, who had escaped that terrible world through self-violent acts, or some quixotic fight with an "overseer" that resulted in death. Wrath had seen that, too. He had occasionally had those visions of an end for himself, too, to bring death to himself amidst the explosion of his fury, but, "No, I live."

At any rate, if he went with this new slave master on his own volition, choosing not to stay and be further humiliated, or possibly being beaten to death at the next act of rebellion, it was rebellion now that was wholly in his soul. "I—I decide…" he said, drawing out the word. "*Use*—countries—all men…against them." He would turn their own works against themselves. It was a last step on Wrath's wretched journey that brought him to the piracy whose deeds would bring further finality. I abuse the word finality, but so many points seem endpoints. After all, Wrath was still alive. His "final" step as pirate would be succeeded by one as prisoner—and, possibly, as an executed man.

24.

It seemed Wrath could not recall the name of the Chinese man, or was it that he could not pronounce it? He conveyed him physically: middle aged and portly—and his persona: he had little of Fukara's satanic fire; but he certainly had his own plans—for which Wrath's talents would prove suitable. As the man's plans would prove suitable for the present pulse of Wrath's psyche.

The Chinese had been like Fukara in that he was as involved with some part of the vast train of refuse, garbage, and discarded artifacts of technological humankind. European firms contracted him to dump their hazardous waste—industrial, even radioactive—in discreet and vulnerable places: land, sea, it didn't matter. Specifically, in the environs of what was once so freely called the Third World, where damaged, divided or at least corrupt governments made this sort of dumping easy. At worst, there was a bit of bribery involved.

But his ships had had a few unprofitable run-ins with the pirates of Somalia, a 21st century version of piracy that the public understood only as a Third World—African—barbarism threatening the just course of modern shipping. But the causes behind this piracy were precisely the factors this allowed this Chinese piratic entrepreneur to do the work he did—and the fact of the work itself: shattered governments, in this case, Somalia, and the dumping of pollutants.

Somalia was a land with a long coastline easy to be bullied (never mind *Blackhawk Down* in Mogadishu in '92). The commercial fishing concerns of many countries had overfished Somali waters, leaving the poor single fisherman of the coast little catch for his own markets and family's sustenance. And pollutants by global concerns and smaller ones (at any rate, foreign) poured their waste into these waters, scarred and denigrated them further, and not only increased the decrease of the maritime food supply, but lapped up on Somali shores: chemicals and, again, radiation, that caused sickness, grave illness, death.

While the Chinese of course, was concerned about his wallet. (At this point, I was having a vision of the man as a bookkeeper type, dry and methodical.) Perhaps he bore too much the psyche of his nation as it leapt into the still new century: at once the most populous country and among the most polluted, its furious pace of industry and modernization in the last quarter of the 20th century spilling into the 21st with all the environmental toxicity that could have been foretold; but the obvious had been largely ignored, perhaps because the communists had deceived themselves to believe pollution endemic only to the misdeeds of the capitalists. A self deception equal to the toxic history of the Soviet Union.

So the Chinese entrepreneur was having his ships of toxic waste either captured, held for ransom (the ship being the worth here, more than the already-paid-for trash), or prevented from reaching their dumping site by having to flee the pirates—who often likened themselves, in fact called themselves, a coast guard. They would not only drive off these foreign invaders, but plunder them. And their blatant industry (eco-friendly, it seemed), actually brought benefits not just to the pirates themselves but many Somalis in general. The pirates spent their ransom money freely, like robber barons boosting the local economy. But they were robbing the world outside of Somalia, which had treated this poor, poor country (75 percent lived on $2 a day) not just with disregard but cruelty. While the pirates almost always treated the crews of the ships they captured with good care; they prized more the ransom than any vengefulness. There were villages, hotels and restaurants that housed and fed the captives—paid for by the pirates. In the meantime, wariness had begun to keep the polluters and the rapacious fishing concerns away. Stocks of fish were growing larger in number. It was a sort of African Robin Hood story.

Not that the pirates were saintly messiahs, or even goodhearted Merryman of English legend. Like men everywhere who may have begun an enterprise in self defense and desperation, success led to excesses: fiefdoms were established with riches, and an attitude that no government rule could ever order them. The government, a bit more patched together now, was trying an uneasy international cooperation, born out of a need for a common defense, brought together authorities of unequal powers and reach to police the coast.

It only made the pirates improve their hardiness and their skills. The pirates had to be—or at least contain within their members—men knowledgeable with the seas, men with the training and attitude of soldiers, and those skilled in the running of ships—and the technology of the modern sea.

The Chinese, not unlike Fukara, had his own vision, his own wild scheme. The problem was that it wasn't coalesced. It was like shards of a mad vision. He thought about creating his own anti-pirates: to keep the pirates from keeping his pollution stymied at sea; and at the same time attacking—and capturing—the ships that international authorities had patrolling the coast to stop the pirates. And he thought about moving piracy to the Pacific, especially along the long chain of islands that comprised Polynesia. He thought of his own African pirates, Wrath among them; he thought of Chinese pirates—and Wrath among them. Telling me this, in his raw, outline way, Wrath stumbled in disdainful difficulties. He had come to understand that grand plans of these men who used and abused Africans were as petty and crazy as they were grand; that in their vast megalomania they were fraught with the ugly vulnerabilities of ego. They came from a damned center of human life, and they were damned to an ugly end.

Chinese pirates, anti-pirates: I would later learn there was a long tradition of Chinese piracy. Two hundred years ago the most successful pirate in history, was Chinese—and a woman. Ching Shih had been a prostitute on a floating brothel off Canton, wed the pirate Cheng I, and, with his death, took over the operation of 1,800 pirate ships and 80,000 men. Contrast that to her contemporary Bluebeard, who commanded four ships and 300 men.

Wrath, polyglot, quick to learn, had several short voyages as an anti-pirate off the coast of Somalia. His ship was sunk by a French cruiser. Some of the pirates drowned, some were captured; Wrath and another made it to shore, hiked some 20 kilometers (Wrath stressed the number, opening wide the fingers of both hands, closing them, opening them again) to a villa base of operations where in casual luxury the Chinese received the two survivors of his vision and almost mocked them for their failure. That was when, as Wrath put it, "I sit down. I say, 'Not this, here.'" He was sitting down metaphorically, I think. His own vision of using the works of other men against themselves was not working out too well. But when the Chinese, in a flippant way, said, "The Pacific, then—" (in what language, I don't know) Wrath, by then perhaps as burdened with his own delusions, illusions, about enacting his psyche upon the world, saw possibilities. It was the vision of ignorance, of course.

In the Pacific, Wrath sailed with a Chinese crew. In months he was proficient in the language; in a year he was in charge of the pirates. It was still a vision that confounded any historical vision of the prejudices of the world: an Asian crew accepting a dark captain. They looted commercial vessels; and they provided a Mafia of the high seas: "protection" for those who sought to make profit by illegally burying in the sea the things that make the planet ill.

It was a time, it was a world of doing that was both burden and freedom for Wrath. The innumerable islands with the vast ocean between them, the island nations that had been truly isolated only a century or so ago and yet even now, in this most modern age, lived so that every horizon held only the sea.

And he came to China, stepped on its soil, this country of one of the oldest civilizations, saw profound fragments of it, the edges if not the center of this vast land that had plenty of pollution with which to sully the world. Wrath, no longer the wretched extractor of metal from burned computer wires, or the insistent traces of gold from circuit boards, was nonetheless still beholden to, still had his existence shaped by the foul effluvia of technology. And there, in China, more than in Africa, he was overwhelmed by the extent of it. The country that houses one fifth of the human race is the world's second largest consumer of pesticides (after the U.S., of course), uses one half of the world's concrete, is the largest producer of steel (guess who was dethroned from Number 1), and is the third largest consumer of oil. As the 20th century closed and spilled into the 21st, China had increased its use of plastic nineteen times in twenty years, while the number of its cars and buses had increased by a factor of fifteen. And as it had increased its production of a First World lifestyle, it had done so even less efficiently than the First World. Three quarters of its energy came from coal, and it has consumed much, much more water than the U.S. and Europe in the production processes of such items as ammonia, used in fertilizer and textile manufacturing.

The dry stats flood in, but they mean visceral things. Deforestation, subsequent erosion, overgrazing by the increasing herds of livestock created by an increasing demand for meat, and 75 percent of its lakes polluted enough to severely affect the health of fish therein. Perhaps most visceral for Wrath, even if his own eyes might now be open to the whole vile spectrum of pollutants, is that China makes a business, an industry out of accepting untreated garbage, chemical wastes and, especially, e-trash. Ships of electronic garbage, 100 tons, 200 tons, more, from other countries are routine at China's ports, resulting in operations like the one I had visited with the crew of *The Argus*.

Anyway, Wrath was seeing at least fragments of vast China, the seas of the Pacific, and he had grown up in the wretched breadth of Africa's e-waste heaps. His world was widening, but so was his perception of the toxic scope of 21st century life. It was a terrible, broadened vision. In a program of piracy that seemed more dreamlike than a day-to-day criminal enterprise, Wrath plundered and racketeered across a vast section of the world, the power and skills of his youth applied to—to what, exactly? Wrath said to me, "Confuse—I couldn't hold—" Perhaps if there had been only one role: pirate, enforcer, shakedown brigand…. Then the thought: "Afraid to make it…only me."

I suppose that meant he was afraid to lose his masters.

But like any skilled criminal henchman, he realized he might have been better rewarded with a larger portion of the spoils he had placed himself on the line to gain. He knew the main part of the "goods" he plundered went to the Chinese—and so there came a time when his sense of, let's say injustice (or we could say the greed of the wrongdoer, too; maybe it was both), a time when he rose up and performed the amazing feat of having his Chinese crew mutiny against their Chinese master. That's something more profound than an African captaining an Asian crew: the black African commanding the allegiance of Chinese against one of their own, appealing to individual greed above natural prejudices There is an unfolding of a venal myth to that that goes beyond psychology. Wrath related the mutiny (he didn't use that word) to me so sparingly it might have been the capture of a foreign, weaker ship—though he himself was capturing a foreign ship, overpowering the weaker psyches of his mates because he had taken a great and strong fury from his life which they had not taken, did not possess from theirs.

It certainly must have astounded the Chinese to see the once beaten Wrath he had taken off Fukara's hands not only successfully usurping him, but having the audacity to attempt it in the first place. But Wrath and mutinous crew were out of reach, literally, at least for a time, on those wonderful, piratical seas—and reveling in the pirates' anxious happiness at keeping all of their bounty.

And in the aftermath of this next step of madness, Wrath and the crew came upon the plastic islands. And Fukara.

26.

"I see crazy things," said Wrath, referring to his first vision—through binoculars—of Arturo Smith's plastic archipelago. "I could *not*..." (his voice fell on the word, expressing how this vision confused him; he could not get the bearings of this reality) "—understand." And he used that word with all its abstract and rich meaning.

Then, almost simultaneously, there was Fukara's ship, docked by Gilligan's Island (of course, Wrath wouldn't know Rita's name for it or that reference); but when Wrath's ship grew closer (I realize now I never asked the name of the pirates' ship—perhaps it was, fittingly, nameless), Wrath's optically aided eye saw Fukara on the deck of *The Gatherer*. In his mind, it all coalesced—not correctly; but again, he couldn't know that. Experience had made him hate Fukara, given him reasons for revenge. Experience had shown him that the Japanese's presence at any surreal operation (and at this point Wrath really had no idea what the plastic islands *were*, except that they were another grotesque setting in which Fukara was surely the focal point) was a mark of evil.

The pirates attacked.

Langhorn—or had it been Smith—or both?—had described it as being an eruption of violence spilling over the plastic islands. Actually, that would have been contrary to the usual procedure 21st century pirates employed. Of course for Wrath this was an event that echoed his name, an event of wrath, not bounty, not material gain. But the pirates did not spill over the island with immediate violence. There was the first, primary exchange between Wrath and Fukara on the deck of *The Gatherer*. A short exchange, but of some moment.

Fukara, certainly surprised and of cautious mockery, greeted Wrath and the Chinese pirates with the guarded expectation that the encounter would become what it did. As for Wrath, he was beyond expectations. For him, the exchange was only to make sure Fukara knew the full extent and powers—and ascendancy—of his soon-to-be executioner. Neither man knew of what the other had been doing since the Chinese had taken the young Wrath from Fukara's e-trash heap; and Wrath could not know that Fukara had come down a bit in the global, labyrinthine world of techno trash. I had found out—and Wrath, too, after his capture—that Fukara's venture of gold extraction from e-trash had been successful enough to gain for him the sort of wealth he could invest—or hide away or both— with one of the companies connected to one of the individuals moving great wealth around the Earth, using it, but adding to it for the investor—until, in some inevitable synchronicity, world markets connected to many things collapsed in a matter of a month, and Fukara's investment company (European) literally went out of existence and the man behind it (I have his name and history somewhere in my notes) committed suicide just before he was about to be arrested (by the police of what country, I am not sure), plunging early one evening from some height of an expensive hotel, leaving behind a large bill. and the sad remains of a splattered human being on the pavement below, shocking the anticipated pleasantries of evening dinner-and theatre-goers. While rumor had it that billions were still sequestered somewhere; but Fukara, with a just a few million to spare, lost most of his e-trash heaps and had been reduced to often being a ferrying middleman for the sort of debris that Arturo Smith would turn into art.

Wrath was saying, "I ask him—he remember. He say, 'You're a man now.' So what happen as child, me, not mean—?" He looked at me with wide, boggling eyes, insisting I agree that Fukara's apparent presumption, that to cast away the past had to be not only crazy but another cruel wound.

"I ask him, 'What this—islands?' He laugh, say, he say—" Wrath tried to rattle his handcuffs to abrade his flesh, to make memory raw. "He say, 'Plastic world. Plastic world art—'"

I thought it indicative of Wrath's mind, his diamond-in-the-rough intelligence, that at least for a moment curiosity preceded murder.

And Fukara's response, the fact of it, the reality of it, added to the deed about to happen.

Wrath babbled a lot more. Wrath the young man had come from the child who had moved with extreme toil up through the world of the trash that had coalesced here, in the midst of the great Pacific, into veritable, atolls, islands, lands. Who knew if, in coming years, there would not be a small continent here? "More crazy—all life—" He tried to string words to make his feelings more precise. It wasn't really necessary. The disjointed words, coming out like cries of splintered emotion, were better than smooth narrative. Even if Fukara had not replied to Wrath's next question, about the girl, his thin lone companion of the e-trash lie, even if Fukara had not answered with, "I never saw her after that night," plainly indicating he had more wanted to deprive Wrath of the girl than had wanted her himself, helping to multiply Wrath's reasons and furies, there still would have been Wrath's furious leap upon Fukara, his strangling the man with his bare hands, the hands that had pulled metal from burning wires, gold from the abraded terrain of circuit boards.

"I think, I not think," said Wrath, looking at me with an expression that might have wanted me to explain to him the state of his emotions when he was killing. As if now, in retrospect, he actually wanted to know the state of his self in that furious moment. Somewhere I'd read or heard that to kill by strangling is the most intimate form of killing. You can't be more than arms length from your victim, and usually you're closer, the arms bent in compressed power, the eyes of the one being strangled fiercely, desperately looking back with the silent scream of something past outrage, fear, or pleas, the whole presence and expression of the victim filling the entire vision of the one who commits this act;—and it seemed to me that Wrath's bare boned outline of the killing of Fukara was itself a face, filling Wrath with the power of the moment: "Body jerk—" Wrath's hands gestured to this side and that. "Sharp—" One word that perfectly caught the abrupt breaking through, the abrupt fall from life to death that Wrath had brought to Fukara.

"I stand, I stand," said Wrath, almost gasping, his own eyes shuttering as if with some violent outside pressure, insistent, almost as if asking me—again—to explain him to himself. I thought: why this word "stand"? To show he was full now, freed of the one who had most abused him in the past? Then again, perhaps Fukara had just been the most obvious abuser, something, yes, a *thing* so blatant it was easy to not fix oneself on all the rest? The abuse of circumstance itself—

The guards, the Nordic and the African, who had stood well enough behind Wrath and had been so still and silent and almost virtually unmoving, at this point stirred, their expressions changed; the fair one stepped forward, the dark one tensed. They were viscerally responding to Wrath's recounting, ready for the possibility that Wrath's anger would grow into an act they would have to subdue.

(As for the Asian that has escorted me into the room: he was no longer there. I realized I had noted his departure soon after bringing me in, but had been so drawn by Wrath's story, I had barely considered that quiet departure.)

But if he was awash with that violence of the past, manacled Wrath would not extend it to anyone in the confines of that room.

Prior to the last encounter with Fukara, Wrath had not been violent. His rebellion against his lot, his declaration to use the sins of others, the self-assured power of others against themselves, had not been a wish for slaughter. Indeed, it had hardly been revenge. It had been a vision that this, now was the best course for himself. He knew enough, he had gleaned enough from his servitude to comprehend the large absurdity— Well, if not comprehend (who does?), then to use it. What is electricity, gravity—or love—for that matter? But we use each, primitive in our artifice, taking phenomena in the way we take the food of Earth. For *none* of us can explain how the palm of the hand can hold several or innumerable seeds, each of which will grow into trees that far outspan us.

But now Wrath had slipped into the next step of "comprehension." Perhaps if he had encountered Fukara again, somewhere other than at the plastic islands, he might have contained violence to that one act. But there, in the midst of the great ocean that should have no mark of humankind, the islands of plastic were a mockery—unnatural seeds, grown larger than himself. To make it more similar: he had held the detritus of plastics in his hands, now he walked on them: techno trash had become the world. A world he could not kill, so he began—or, rather, after killing Fukara he continued—to strike out at those who had worked this world into largeness.

"Another—man—I—"

"Killed?"

"Not know." The eyes weren't as extraocular, more inward. His manacled arms made weird gestures. As if they could not—at least now—coordinate with his recent fury. His recent...wrath.

So one act of murder led him to another violence in which he had been so blinded he could not now say if the result had been murder or not.

What he didn't say, what he could describe only obliquely, was that the Chinese pirates he led, who apparently had more violence in them, took signal from Wrath's slaying of Fukara and enacted their own aggressions on the inhabitants of the plastic islands. Wrath related how one of the pirates killed a man: "Island—big face—he fell from eyes—" From the giant half visage of computer monitors. I heard nothing about the death of Alfredo, who had sought completion of the ziggurat, the structure whose origins had been used to raise bloody sacrifices closer to the sky.

27.

He was silent; I was, too. We looked at each other almost peacefully. It seemed the guards had relaxed. Their expressions were truly inscrutable. While Wrath cocked his head; the slightest smile floated there, like a slim ship on a vague sea. And then there was the recognition—again (I was aware of it, like seeing a distant flag on a precise horizon)— that he and I shared ancestors from the same continent, but I, apart from that land, had lived the better life, while he had had to persevere through what had been taken from him.

So much had been—outlined; and said within the unsaying spaces. This young man was going toward some long imprisonment or even execution at some international hand: the quasi-authority of a New World Order, you could call it. He certainly had the extenuating circumstances of his life to present to any court, to present as mitigating circumstance, his having been one of the sad millions—billions—one of the wretched of the Earth, the 21st century's oppressed man, descended from immemorial centuries of intentional, callous cruelties, product of histories of a colonialism and global garbage and the countryless psyche of the scattered beings of a continent. His life might inspire pity, and even leniency. But he would not be granted freedom. Nor surcease. Perhaps prison would be a surcease: captivity, but no—or only a little—toil. And then—assuming no death sentence—perhaps a release in old age, at least much older than now, in the future's decades, in some science fictional mid century, and he would step into a world that— Oh, I wondered at that future myself. To someone in the middle of the last century, say in 1950 or 1960, the mark, the number of this year in which I'd voyaged through a plastic sea would seem the limits of imagination, a time when so much would have been altered and even an apocalypse rendered. And yet I think the truth is that even a half century changes things less than those at the beginning of that half century would have imagined. Oh, we have instantaneous global communication now, we have genome decoding and cloning and the apocalypse of garbage, etc., etc., but the human heart, its bounties and depravities: timeless. So aged Wrath will step out into a decade technology has further changed and shaped, but where the same venalities and graces reside. And he will know that mirror and know it defeated him. And walk in that sorrow through the rest of his days— But will he be weighed with sorrow then? Or, just, acceptance? Or will he have left those hard emotions, left them before or during imprisonment, or before killing, or even farther back, in the toil of a child somewhere in Africa, picking from the debris of human artifacts something of false, fleeting worth? And live out the life of flesh so long, so very long after the spirit has been subsumed in the life here, the life that demands spiritlessness, in which the spirit must battle each instant to survive as fact and continue as domain?

*   *   *

It was almost with afterthought that I asked Wrath about being pursued, his dive into the waters of the Great Garbage Patch, his entanglement with the diaphanous plastic. He looked at me a little surprised, as if recovering from such a depth of interior thought that he could not make the transition to any other moment in his life. Or perhaps the trauma of his end of the road, so to speak (strange choice of words for the ocean, but it is a sort of roadway, broad, vast, vast enough to choose any number of "paths"—in other words, a place for journeys), perhaps those moments of capture had so stunned him that he looked to them through a mist of—denial?

No, he didn't deny. He got to it, if slowly. "We go on," he said, and I realized he had hardly—if ever—referred to a "we" in any part of his story. He had always been a being alone. It had always been himself, the boy Wrath, the young man Wrath, against the world. He had never been part of a "we."

But now—at least in that moment—fleeing criminals, having committed murder and assault, mayhem and ravaging—in that Wrath slipped into "we." Well, there is a solidarity among criminals. Some criminals. Within the absurd moments of some crimes. Of the illusions of self-deception. Vile natures, expressed in concert, if discordantly, and the illusions of a sort of bond, even if the illusion is brief. But even as Wrath spoke this, I believed he saw through the fallacy of that single word, that group pronoun; he had been the force behind and before the Chinese pirates; to say "we" was almost a lie.

For when he saw himself trapped by the vessels of the UN authorities, he said, with great passion, "I didn't want— They *hold* me. I—*this*—" He gestured to his captors, his two jailers, his two guards, stolid and ever ready, nearby, blinking back at him without expression. Again I had to remind myself they were present. They were essentially self-effacing observers as much as jailers. Or did they even care they saw? Care *what* they saw? What they heard? Their only prompt the possibility of the truculence of a prisoner. Their bland, stolid presence derived power from the power that the pirate Wrath had seen closing in on him, and which had made him dive, in doomed escape, into the great, garbage-violated Pacific.

I said, simply, even with sympathy, "You thought that was escape?"

He looked back at me with—was it anger? How could I know his feelings, his dilemma? He didn't respond. But told me, with blunt resignation: "Something—around—could not see— Then I could—*plastic* net—" He put an emphasis on "plastic" that made it a profanity. A portion of the trash that had been his world had engulfed him, snared him. He didn't seem to express this with any horror, he didn't seem to have felt horror then, as most of us would have, being dragged under, then, pushing himself up, against the plastic thing and the water, the great artificial jellyfish clinging tighter, though, and then down again, ultimately and in short order being rescued by his pursuers, hauled up to a bright, sun-steamy deck, the struggled trapped insect in a giant cocooned web that was not animate and yet wrapped and twisted itself about him as if life indeed.

He did not mention being shot in the arm, that minor wound being lost in the greater threat of that plastic aberration.

Then there flowed from him this sad grace of revelation—resignation. Sighing, he said, "I rest then—stop.... End." (He made that short word the ultimate echo of surrender.) "They—cut it—away...." He said something about a thick knife glinting in the sun. He was stripped from his trap, gasping and soaked on the deck, the faces of many nations looking down on him, like a sampling of the world in which he had been violated—and then, in response, had himself violated. Bodies pressed about him, dark commanding silhouettes in the sun; then he was bound again, with thick, wet rope.

*   *   *

Before I left, I did ask him, "Did it feel alive?"

Those bugged out eyes blinked. He said, "Sometimes the computers—I feel—butcher like to animals—"

What was he talking about? "Computers are already dead. Always dead."

He squinted in denial. "Electricity through them. Life."

"I meant that plastic—net."

"Oh," he nodded. "Jellyfish."

"Yes, like that. Alive?"

"Soft, almost couldn't see. But—but—"

"Insistent," I offered. He squinted again, at this word that puzzled him a moment. I said, "Didn't give up."

He shook his head, not as a negative sign, but one of incomprehension. "In water—I see—it did not end— Far to the end of the water."

"They cut into it—to get you."

"Yes."

"Like a birth. A womb." I was being a bit way out, but it also seemed fitting.

Again the squint. Well, he may have thought I was being crazy. His response was, "My parents dead. AIDS—they tell me."

Why was he saying that again? I guess I had prompted him, with "womb." "Yes, you said. You were already born—before."

The Asian who had brought me in came back into the room, as if he had been listening to all of this and knew—or decided—this was the end of the interview. I found out later he was Vietnamese. I wondered, even though that war is decades gone now, what was the attitude of most Vietnamese toward most Americans. Well, he would not have been alive then, or just barely so, and I hadn't been, so….

I pushed my chair back. Wrath tilted his head back to watch me as I rose. I nodded to him. He blinked, drew in a long breath. His time with me had been an effort. –Another necessary step in the struggle of his life?

I left him, filled so much with his tale, but with so much unsatisfied, as the truth of what life is here dissatisfies us, with the guards escorting me back out into the bright light of day, perhaps patronizingly, believing they held more knowledge than what I thought I had seen—and heard. They were—are—wrong. I know—now: Something.

28.

My adventures on the journey of *The Argus* have changed my perceptions. Or not so much changed them as sharpened perceptions already in place.

I was in a thrift store recently—though it could have been any type of store that bore this subsequent vision: The clothes on the racks, the shoes, the books on shelves, the computers and leaf blowers and children's toys (most of them plastic) were to my eyes one step away from the garbage heap—be it the Sargasso of the Great Garbage Patch at sea, or the e-trash heaps of China and Africa (and surely we have our own e-trash heaps somewhere). It was so easy to imagine this bright red and yellow plastic tricycle swirling slowly on that great ocean, traveling endlessly on the currents, the clothing made ragged with weather, its strands of fabric laced into the dirt of landfills like the strata of some bacteria. Just too many *things*....

Which I especially thought about regarding the books. The thoughts of so many people, made up stories, histories true or embellished, the vast, vast majority worthless—though of course that's subjective. Victor Hugo next to some bestseller of five years past that was made into a TV movie. Isn't there something in the Bible—*Ecclesiastes*?—to the effect that there is no end to the writing of books? Of course, I want to think *my* account is of worth.

And perhaps the vision was more pertinent in a thrift shop. Goods, already used, to be used again—a first glance that's good, right? On the other hand, this was the last stop for these items, these trinkets and tools and entertainments of our civilization before they became garbage. Too much, too much. A civilization of things, distractions and objects—to keep us from...what? If each of us could see the end of it, as I had....

Or had I seen only penultimate things? There is the feeling that all I have witnessed is only a herald (that word I've used almost naively) for something more revelatory of existence and even doom.

At any rate, am I changed, will I use less? Will I, who has had intimacy with the e-trash heaps of continents and plastic cluttering the ocean be more circumspect in regard to this world of perpetually manufactured things? I will, I will—I do. But life here demands…a certain self-violation. Yes, that's what I've learned. To live at all one *accepts*: one can't avoid a certain degree of debasement. Those with the knowledge—and the will—keep that debasement minimal, but isn't it, ultimately, only a matter of degree, not of kind? There is the basis of so many faiths: the instinct pointing to the fact that to live here, to choose to survive here, is a sin.

*   *   *

One hot day I saw pallets of plastic water bottles being unloaded outside of a store. The towers of bottles were in turn wrapped in tight plastic. They sat in the sun. The heat of the plastic wrap and the plastic of the bottles themselves soaked in this solar heat—so surely more of the BPA, a proven hormone disruptor, in the plastic would be released into the water. Later—it could be within hours—someone would drink this water, after the bottles had been brought inside and chilled, and the cool water would satisfy the drinker on this hot day, the poisons consumed unnoticed. And in some near future the bottles could be floating on an ocean, slightly deteriorating, again warmed with the sun. Haven't I said that every single bit of plastic ever made is still in existence? Even if in the smallest parts—like the net of possibly replicating plastic tinged with the warp of Fukushima's ocean-borne radioactivity, the myth-like beast we encountered in the travels of *The Argus*, the

beast-creature whose portions Rory studies, with the hope that
the monster was, is, alive?

*   *   *

Before it was aired, Melissa invited me to see a cut of her
documentary. In a small screening room in a Manhattan
skyscraper, I watched Melissa's vision of the voyage—though
certainly Blaise's vision was there, too. There was the heroic
and often curmudgeonly Hurston, dutiful Jorges and Emile,
Rita and myself, and of course Rory—who might be the
Professor on *Gilligan's Island*. After Rita had dubbed Smith's
plastic island with that name, I couldn't shake a foolish
connection to that farce made before I was born.

Like a lot of people, I was not comfortable seeing myself on
camera, but I won't say any more about that.

Hurston was at the screening, greeting both of us soberly,
even with an awkward reserve—as if he now felt he'd been too
familiar with us during the voyage, that he'd allowed us to see
too deep below his skin. Or, perhaps more likely, as if about to
see, to witness, the aspects of that voyage that had been so far
from his control.

I had wondered how Melissa would handle all the
strangeness that had crowded into the voyage—Arturo Smith
and the plastic islands, the mannequin and the Buddhas, the
bizarre plastic thing in the sea, the pirate Wrath. To her credit
she did it straightforwardly. Halfway through the film the
viewer was experiencing a journey that the beginning of the
story had not in the least anticipated. I was especially taken by
the surreal images of the plastic islands: it gave the impression
of explorers coming upon an utterly new land—a new
continent, you could say. And the juxtaposition, later on, of
their ruins, the ravaging of the small, unreal society. Equally
surreal but much more moving was the funeral at sea of Emile,

that first ceremony, without his body. I had forgotten Melissa had not had Blaise film that second funeral, when we did return his weighted body to the sea.

The documentary grew into a strange, existential horror film: the ghostly plastic thing that was almost not there—there was a shot of this vaguest of shimmering stretched across the sea, lost just before the horizon; then a few seconds with Rory with a portion of the thing in a pan of water, holding up a smaller portion in a test tube, the mad dreamer of a scientist believing in the possibility of the fantastic, explaining the potential of semi-animate replication from plastic. This would perhaps be the least realistic portion of the film to the average viewer, who would be much more stricken by the ubiquity of plastic waste clogging the oceans, and the e-trash heaps of China—rendered, I have to say, with full apocalyptic power. (If not allowed to film there, Melissa had used Blaise's drawings to full effect. Their starkness was actually more striking than video might have been.) The century that had seen human beings go from riding horses to piloting mooncraft, had segued into the century of a stagnancy into which the planet's creative species was slave to its own creations. But because I had lived the story, Rory with that test tube struck me with an inner disturbance equal to anything else in this untoward adventure.

I do have to say this one thing about watching myself in that documentary. In trying to be as much an observer as Melissa and Blaise, I was not recorded as much as the rest of the crew, but the aspect that was brought to me when I was, gave me more than a passing thought (a thought I'd had before, reinforced) that I was a black person recording an odd voyage of white people aided by the apparently menial but invaluable efforts of hired Mesoamericans. It's sometimes impossible to lift oneself past racial divisions.

Afterwards, in that small dark room abruptly relit, Melissa nodded at me with a satisfied smile. I Could not help acquiescing to her satisfaction; I said, "Well, it worked."

Melissa's smile spread further with self congratulation. "You—the others—thought I couldn't do—that."

I was tactful. "You went beyond—clichés." Then I quickly said: "Did it change you? It must have."

Perhaps she didn't want to answer that question, so she threw it back. "Did it change you?"

"Well, going through all that—" I said something which I can't remember now, all the while wondering if the voyage of *The Argus* had not so much changed me (as it had certainly wrought something new in Melissa) as affirmed a perspective—you could even call it a foreboding—my persona, my psyche, had always possessed. Or suffered under.

I said, finally, simply, "Of course. It changed all of us."

Melissa blinked those gemstone eyes—and almost, imperceptibly, nodded.

Hurston, deep in some silence, blew out a breath and said, "It's true: a journey—a voyage—takes you…somewhere else. Not necessarily the place you thought you were going." Perhaps he was convincing himself to accept that truth.

Melissa's documentary also showed scenes taken after I'd left *The Argus* to interview Wrath. There was one moment in the film—probably no more than ten or fifteen seconds—that was, well, ironic? At least sadly fitting. After the inundation of the floating Buddhas I think it was Rita who remarked something about finding a floating Christ next. And so, captured in Blaise's omnipresent eye, was none other than Hurston extracting with slow wariness and seeming wonder a small object from a morass of things Rory had fished from the ocean: a small plastic crucifix, the lean naked body upon it a mass-produced item of faith, shining slightly with the wetness from which it had been raised up. Hurston looked down at it sadly, like a man contemplating the symbol of a sacrifice that was incomprehensible, or simply the artifact of an incomprehensible belief.

Hurston, watching this alongside me, said, "I threw it back into the water."

"You didn't want to keep it?"

He shrugged. "I don't like symbols."

"You're a bit of a symbol now yourself," I said, somewhat inanely.

He squinted at me, the way he'd squinted across the Pacific to so many horizons. "No.... Just someone trying to show everyone—something."

Then I suddenly remembered: I was the one who had made the comment about coming across a floating Christ next. I guess it seemed more like something Rita would have said.

Anyway, I thought: flung back onto that sea, the crucifix would probably not be picked up by anyone else again. In a century or so it would be degraded enough to wind up in the bellies of fish, an ironic end for the symbol of the one who proclaimed himself a fisher of men.

Fisher of men—fishing nets—the glimmering. Recently, driving by a beach, I saw a man on a stone jetty toss a fishing net into the water, the dark grid of netting unfurling and ruffling in the wind. The netting meant to bring fish to their deaths, and which was pushing the sea to its death; and, bringing, eventually, death to us. I drove on, imagining trapped fish banging against the rocky jetty with the pull and tearing of the currents, while the man who had cast the net was apart from any such brooding.

After the screening Hurston abruptly said, "That ship—*The Gatherer*—nobody ever found it?"

Melisa: "Haven't heard anything about it. It's down in all that plastic, I guess."

Hurston seemed thoughtful. "Maybe I'll go find that next." Then he smiled, to show he really couldn't be serious. Maybe.

Melissa laughed. "Let me know. That'll be a good epilogue."

Or another strange odyssey for that man, if he wants to curse himself further, I thought. It seemed to me Hurston's smile and laugh were a disguise of intent.

*   *   *

As for Arturo Smith, he did stay on, among his ruined, giant artwork; and Langhorn remained with him, becoming, through trauma and sympathy, an aid, even a worker in the creation— the re-creation—of the archipelago. Catastrophe had joined the two. Smith would soon say he was incorporating the pirates' depredations into the idea—or ideal—of the work as a whole. "Some of the ruins will be left. We don't want to rebuild the Coliseum." So Smith was the glory that was Rome and the Renaissance, too, after the Dark Ages. In fact, when he saw the giant ravaged, computer monitor head with its half visage, he said he loved it even more than the original; and if the ziggurat is being completed, the graffiti, profane or otherwise, will remain. At its height Smith plans a mural depicting Alfredo.

As for Hurston's original aim. Well, he certainly had gathered enough data to preach about—to be fair I should say: instruct—the need to turn from this incessant production that has become a plague of marine detritus. He would talk about this all over the world. Though I am sure there were things he had learned during the voyage of *The Argus* that he could not really communicate. Some discoveries are too personal to extend beyond oneself.

Rory Chapman went into the silence of sequestered research immediately after the voyage, though I think we'll know soon if he proclaims the discovery of anything resembling replicating plastic. I have the indelible images of Emile drowning in the glimmering—and the image I did not personally see, but which was related rawly enough, of the Somali trying to escape within it, ensnared by its 21st century surface. The wrath of Wrath in our violated sea…. While Jorges, perhaps more the survivor than any of us, who had given forth with those reflexive reverences, now crosses himself (at least figuratively) in simple appreciation that he is safe once more. He returned to the Hamptons, where the only horror at sea is the collage of bland faces with banal demands emerging into vision, then lost, during those parties on their yachts.

29.

I was drawn to Wrath's fate again by learning he now had an unusual legal representative. He was to be tried before The Hague for piracy and murder. His attorney came from a world not dissimilar to his, though hardly one as brutal. She, yes, *she*, was from Somalia, and that was noteworthy in itself. As Wrath, she had been orphaned, her parents dying in their twenties, either victims of jihadists or jihadists themselves, a fact never determined, as she herself admitted, on a BCC interview I saw. Aasiya Belawa was a striking woman (cliché, but it fit), whose life had been saved and nurtured by western aid workers who had come upon her in a makeshift orphanage. She had been adopted by a French diplomatic family and educated in Paris and so had been given a European resurrection. Thus, like Wrath, she had come from hard beginnings, but, very unlike her client, she had been rescued into a much easier world. The interview she gave made plain how much she realized this, and had pledged herself to help the much less fortunate (another cliché that fitted).

Her name bespoke of Somalia's layered history. In ancient times the Land of Punt, this people of the Horn of Africa had been a trading link between the Orient (as we used to say) and the West. Invaded by Arabs who now worshipped Allah, and then in more recent times by the French, Italians and British, the modern world had allowed Somalia its independence in 1960. "Aasiya" is Arabic for "a means to help the weak." That had indeed been her given name at birth, as if a coincidence the future had planned. She had taken "Belawa" as a Somali name with a purpose: it is a sword. In the interview she had remarked, "As when Jesus said in your Gospels, 'I came not to bring peace but a sword,'" adding, "I need to cut through what has wounded so many."

I said she was striking and could—as others had remarked— easily have been a model as a lawyer. She had a dark regal face that would have been received as an exotic beauty in the West; but, I thought, there was something too profound and even old in her aspect, her expression, for her to be bound to nothing other than the path she chose. Her features, her face, so African, seemed to possess all the visceral knowing, of remembrance of centuries of suffering under the colonialism of Europeans and Arabs; it knew a burden that had to be expiated. –A visage that had not only seen this history, but bore an all too modern travail; this Somali woman might well have been in those photos and videos Hurston had showed us, a woman with sooted face and body, and an expression both indomitable and resigned, moving among her kindred toiling through the e-trash of this new century. Heritage and circumstance had chosen her for her present task as "Third World champion."

It was from that interview I also learned she would use not only Wrath's harsh life path as mitigating circumstances for his defense, but his present physical condition. I had noted the bugged out eyes that indicated a thyroid condition, but Belawa had gone further. Prompted by his continual youthful exposure to the toxic world of e-waste, she had pushed for a thorough examination of Wrath, which had discovered—and certainly it couldn't be a surprise—not merely the entire eco-system of his body violated by plastic particles, but his brain itself. His so-called seat of reason had been invaded by not only plastic nanoparticles but literal plastic fibers as well. I envisioned thread-like plastic fibers that could be extracted from the pathways of neurons and synapses, a violation of the weave of the engine of the mind. Perhaps this was the ultimate postcolonial desecration, through the plastics that had been invented by the West. Belawa would argue that this utter desecration of mind and body had poisoned him to the extent that he could hardly be held fully responsible for his actions.

Not that she expected a verdict of innocence. The interviewer, a youngish woman both intent and sympathetic, who had also grown up with the benefits of western life and education, but had been born into this safety, and perhaps couldn't help not having a full sympathy toward Wrath when considering his crimes, had pressed Belawa on the matter of Wrath's guilt. Belawa replied, "I will not say he was *controlled* by the pollution he has suffered, but that he's been bound by it. It's as if every step you take, you are tied by a rope to something very bad."

"But you are always able to cut the rope?" the interviewer asked, as if a suggestion that had not been considered.

Belawa paused, then said, "You perhaps do not know you can cut the rope. And, if you do...you are not so much freed as...confused before a world that won't have you in any way."

The interviewer cocked her head at that; I do not recall her response or further questions, but I noted she sipped from a plastic water bottle. I am now forever haunted by the presence of such plastic, toxic agents we have let loose in our lives.

At any rate, I had to consider Wrath in a further light: early 21st century man, disparaged flesh encasing a plastic invasion. I still had to believe that the wrath of Wrath had to be so much more than the oppressiveness of his virtual captivity and his toil, of his psyche being more violated by the evil of humans than the invasion of plastic, but: if we go at this pace, if we can, as Rory had hoped (or rather posited), recycle to the point at which the literal presence of plastic does not increase, the end of this century may bring us billions of humans not, as we have been lately wont to envision, to a time living with a melding of flesh and biotechnology, but infested with the parasites of the plastic polymers whose history Rory had outlined to me, a history begun by unrelated inventers, separated in time and intent, who certainly could not have foreseen this present world. The true plastic islands will be settled archipelagos in the neural oceans of the mind. *This* could be the replicating plastic life—our creation taken truly inland, our pathways to thought synthetic polymers.

I recalled that Wrath, like Emile, had been engulfed in the glimmering plastic in the midst of the vast Pacific. Wrath had survived to face his crimes. I wondered if that almost supernatural glimmering had, at that moment, wrapped itself about a being it "saw" as not so different than itself, another entity of the plastic world. We had rescued Wrath from that grasp, but, as we drag him among us, it should be recognized that the world we thrust upon him made him a tortured hybrid condemned to a borderline so many of us can't recognize, yet which marks the territories of a war in which too many do not apprehend the nature of the enemy we ourselves have placed against us.

30.

I was reviewing all this right after the World Health Organization declared the new virus a pandemic and I was watching scenes of a locked down Wuhan concurrent with normal life being locked down in the United States. It wasn't that odd seeing the Chinese in masks, they'd often worn them during times of various flu outbreaks and to combat the pollution of their cities, but this was a new turn for Americans. Those who have so far deigned to wear them, at least. There was the expected resistance. I figured this virus would be with us for a few months; I wondered how serious it would get, how Americans would deal with it. Americans do not like to be restricted.

Of course, in regard to China, I recalled their e-trash heaps. And thought about how all those masks, and the medical gloves, both there and in America, will add to the human-created waste of Earth. I sadly imagined those masks and gloves soon gathering a presence in the Great Pacific Garbage Patch.

So the dream—nightmare—I had wasn't unexpected.

I was struggling in the seas of the glimmering, that gelatinous mass seeking (yes, as if with conscious intent) to draw me under. I felt the victim of a purpose. At the same time, I felt my head breached, invaded, the plastic seeping into my brain, as it had violated Wrath's brain—his in the fires of the landbound e-trash heaps, mine in the seas clogged with the pollution the land could not hold. For the longest, painful moments, I felt my mind battered with the circumstance of two minds, the mind that was mine, and the mind of the invader, with "thoughts" that were indecipherably inhuman, that could not be related: a message—an insistence—of an alien presence.

My body and my mind were both being drowned. Like a being on the verge of being murdered, I had a final burst of strength; my head, almost parallel to the surface of the water, broke just above it. I gasped and screamed. It was a wordless scream—that was quickly stifled by a medical mask that suddenly floated on my face, across my mouth. I choked, I gasped; the water closed over my face; the mask floated above me, like an inanimate disguise that would efface me.

They say you can't dream that you actually die; I awoke with a jolt, blood thundering in my throat. I sat up in bed for a few minutes, closing my eyes against the dark room, closing them to the vision of the dream. I wondered, in that darkness, if the terrible sensation of my mind being invaded was something like what Wrath had felt—still feels. Though when I had interviewed him, he'd given no indication of experiencing such an invasion. Perhaps the parasitic plastic had become a normal part of his being—the invader an aspect of the everyday.

The next day I was reading online accounts of the protective medical gear that the pandemic necessitated, and again I thought of it all, in a few months' time, or years, becoming a new violation of the Earth.

And thought, as news of this never experienced lockdown in America moved across our immediate days, that the safest place in a plague would be out at sea—if you had left land before the contagion had taken hold. I gave myself a wry inner smile at that. I hadn't thought myself neither safe nor endangered (well, for the most part) during the strange voyage I'd undergone, but now I looked on this so recent passage with a nostalgia that surprised me, and regarded those days with an irony that was almost longing.

But there was certainly danger now. I had been the observer of worldwide pollution, but my dream had brought to me the very personal danger of the aggregate of so many things that had been created without a thought that the sheer exponential flood of their production threatened my very own life.

The sperm count of men in the western world has dropped 59 percent since the early 1970s. At this rate, half the men in the west will be infertile by some time in this century. The culprit: the hormone disruptors in plastics. Ubiquitous plastic has also caused an 80 percent rise in miscarriages. Whether the non-western world has been less or more or equally affected, we don't yet know. But we may very well be looking at a future in which human beings can't reproduce, at least not without extensive technological help. —And will there be human stud farms, with fertile males the true sex symbols of this coming dystopia?

Want more visual proof? Boys are being born with smaller penises. The result of the Faustian bargain in which we so embraced plastic will have this as irrefutable, graphic evidence.

The human race, rendered extinct, by plastic water bottles....

And, in millennia hence, the extraterrestrials from wherever will find the expected ruins, but, even more prevalent, the synthetic polymer morass that subsumed us, hardly noting the much degraded but still existing Buddhas and crucifixes of the Great Pacific Garbage Patch, remnants of that effluvia of faith that will not even be recognized as such.

*   *   *

And then a final—or actually the most recent—thought on all this: I had connected Wrath's tragedy to a sort of technological post-colonial horror. But why hadn't I made that connection with Emile? His people had come from a joining of conquerors and the conquered. And more importantly, why hadn't I made that connection with my own heritage? My ancestors had been brought from one continent to another, across an ocean, chained in ships—and, on that foreign shore, sold as beasts of burden. How many sins have our seas seen? I repeat that alliteration with sad irony. We have placed so much sadness upon these waters.

My own father had been hunted on the streets of America because he had opposed that centuries-long heritage of captivity: even hunted at times by his own race, made so bitter through generations that they saw in their reflections an enemy; hunted along with that oppressing other, the heirs to the conqueror. And now I am free to write of what may slay us all, in a manner so unlike other invasions we can't quite comprehend it. And the cry of my words may be a cry that will be too long ignored.

www.ingramcontent.com/pod-product-compliance
Lightning Source LLC
Chambersburg PA
CBHW020943180626
46814CB00003B/910